A. DORMAN LEISHMAN

CAPTAIN TALBOT'S RECKONING

Complete and Unabridged

LINFORD
Leicester

First published in Great Britain in 2011 by
Robert Hale Limited
London

First Linford Edition
published 2013
by arrangement with
Robert Hale Limited
London

British Library CIP Data

Leishman, Anne Dorman.
Captain Talbot's reckoning. - -
(Linford western library)
1. Western stories.
2. Large type books.
I. Title II. Series
823.9′2–dc23

ISBN 978–1–4448–1491–0

Published by
F. A. Thorpe (Publishing)
Anstey, Leicestershire

Set by Words & Graphics Ltd.
Anstey, Leicestershire
Printed and bound in Great Britain by
T. J. International Ltd., Padstow, Cornwall

This book is printed on acid-free paper

CAPTAIN TALBOT'S RECKONING

Captain Nathan Talbot lost almost everything in the late Civil War, including his self-respect and his honour. Now, living in a quiet backwater — thinking his days of notoriety are over — an unexpected bequest brings him to the Saville ranch. But the Saville family, already suffering a crippling loss because of Nathan Talbot, are in deep trouble. As he gets nearer to the truth about who is trying to destroy Gregory Saville, he comes closer to his own personal reckoning.

To the one and only Jean

1

In the shade of the station waiting-room, Nathan Talbot watched the faces of the men who had come to kill him. He watched them with the dull curiosity of someone who no longer cared and when he had seen all he wanted to see, he turned and leaned his back against the wooden framework of the building, folding his arms and staring without seeing at the clutter of shacks across the railroad tracks.

He had been warned about these men by one of the few friends he had in this town but Talbot had not been very deeply disturbed by the news, for he had long known that there were people who cared enough to seek him out, even in as far-flung a corner as this one. He was surprised, though not at all flattered, that whoever wanted him to die had felt the necessity of sending two men. But not surprised that someone wanted him dead. He had been expecting that for some years now.

He lowered the brim of his hat a fraction and moved out of the shade into brittle sunlight, the heat striking him a dull, flat blow across the shoulders. He turned his head towards the two of them and, coolly, they looked back. A realist, Talbot knew there was no point in staying to fight it out, knew that he could never hope to outgun a gunman, even a second-rate gunman. And apparently, the slim angular one in the cheap dark suit came with something of a reputation. Besides which, Talbot had not carried a gun since the war.

He knew the gunman's name was Castle, that he was from Savannah, with a courteous southern gentlemanliness, his informant had said, that belied the fact that he had the disposition of a rattlesnake. His friend, with the mop of curly, boyish hair and face of raddled granite, a man of immense physical strength, was named simply Billy. Billy's presence along with Castle made Talbot wonder if they had plans for him other than shooting. He blinked and then looked away from them, closing his eyes as sweat from his brow stung his eyelids, the heat pulsing heavily against the closed lids.

This was the first opportunity Talbot had given the two men to take a look at their target. He was tall and his shoulders had a healthy span under a faded but clean, dark-blue work shirt. His eyes were brown and the eyes were the clue to the man. They were full of wreckage. His hair was black and needed cutting and his accent, heard by Castle earlier when he bought his train ticket, betrayed him as an easterner. He was a very good-looking man and Castle thought him an interesting mark, for he was obviously quality, but jaded and gone to seed. It was also obvious that he knew they were following him. Castle glanced at Billy, faintly annoyed because he suspected that it was this slow-witted, ox of a man who had given them away.

'Train comin',' Billy said, ignoring his partner's look and his words were punctuated by a long, shrill whistle. The loose group of people on the platform began to sort themselves out, gathering luggage, drifting towards the rails. Talbot stooped to lift his leather grip, running his finger over the mono-grammed initials with the reflex of habit.

Three days ago he had received a letter from a lawyer in New York telling him that a cousin of his father's had left him a half-share in a ranch. Cousin Lyle, who had lived in New York and who had never been further west than the Algonquins, had died recently without offspring. Nathan had been the closest thing he had to a son. Talbot had been intrigued less by his cousin's bequest than how those lawyers had tracked him down. But he wouldn't have gone looking for an answer if Castle and Billy hadn't shown up. Now there seemed little point in staying on in this part of the world and that half-share suddenly looked a brighter prospect than a brutal finish on a quiet street one night. And he was pretty sure he could lose those two along the way.

He had packed his grip this morning, quit his job at the livery stable and bought a ticket at the railroad station. The man who had warned him about Castle had come to see him off. He was the town sheriff.

'Just came to see you made it here all right.' Sheriff John Wells was a little taller than Talbot, his hair and eyes a warm, sandy colour, his face creased with the sun and a lifetime of hunting down men like the two who stood at the other end of the platform. He gave the pair of them a long, knowing, lawman's stare, then wrung Talbot's hand with customary vigour and searched into the mildly smiling face for clues to this very odd business.

'I've got this feeling I'll not be seeing you again.'

'I thought officers of the law didn't have feelings,' Talbot said lightly.

'Can't find a thing on either of those two in any of my fliers, but I've wired the US marshal, just to see if he has anything. Till I get a reply I can put them away, just long enough to let you get clear.'

He nodded towards the two deputies he had brought along, who stood off to one side, waiting for a pre-arranged signal. Talbot shook his head.

'I'm not about to stand still and let them kill me,' he responded, a touch of exasperation in his voice.

'You'll be on that train till almost dark. That's long enough for them to try something.'

'Not on a crowded train. Not with witnesses.'

'You have to get off the train sometime,' Wells pointed out. 'What then?'

'I'll think of something. Anyway, maybe it isn't me they're after. Maybe your informant got it wrong.'

'No,' Wells shook his head gravely. 'You've been expecting them. I saw it in your face when I told you. I know you're not wanted by the law. I checked. I just wish you trusted me enough to tell me what it is they want you for.'

The smile faded from Talbot's face and he turned away to watch as the train drew into the station, venting steam and causing a flurry of activity around them.

'I owe some people,' he said, turning back to look at his friend, smiling again but this time without strength or conviction.

'And Castle and Billy have come to collect?'

'Something like that.'

Wells had been puzzling over the why of it for days. What had this easygoing, educated, unassuming man done to warrant the attentions of a heartless killer like Castle?

'Will you let me know when you get there? Just a line or a telegram, let me know you're still in one piece?' Talbot nodded briefly that he would, shook hands again and boarded the train. He took a seat near the front of the carriage and sat down, raising a hand in salute as the train pulled slowly away past the sheriff.

Wells glared at the two men who had seated themselves further back. He would remember them if anything were to happen to his friend. A brave man or maybe just a fool. Perhaps it was just that Talbot had nothing left to lose.

2

For a while, as the train curved across the semi-desert terrain south of town, he speculated on the letter. He had cut all ties during the war, with family, with friends. His father was dead. He had not seen his sisters or his mother since sixty-three and he had not met James Lyle for ten years or more. Lyle had been a businessman, sharper than Talbot's very shrewd father and with interests in almost every field, including, as it now turned out, cattle. How Lyle had come to own a half-share in a ranch thousands of miles from the safety and respectability of New York, Talbot did not know. All he did know was that he was headed for the Velarde ranch and that the train would bring him within a few miles of it early that evening.

Before the war, his father had been

priming him to take over the family shipping and freight business and, like a lot of men who had been through the crucible of war, he had acquired a variety of skills, but he knew absolutely nothing about cattle ranching. It puzzled him for a while that Lyle should leave him such a strange bequest but soon the emptiness of these speculations wearied him and he slept.

He awoke late in the afternoon, roused by the voices of two men who had been playing cards behind him and now were beginning to quarrel. Talbot blinked and looked out of his own window at rolling prairie grasses and a wavering purple haze on the distant hills.

The carriage had been full at the start of the journey and had not thinned out much. The passengers were restless now, talking amongst themselves as the argument between the poker players began to take on an edge of seriousness.

Talbot twisted around in his seat to

take a look and saw that they were almost directly between himself and his two shadows. Suddenly the quarrel erupted into a blistering fight, both men on their feet, swinging wildly at one another, effectively blocking him from sight.

He recognized that this was probably the only opportunity he would have of losing Castle and Billy. He reached quietly for his grip, which was on the floor between his feet and, unobtrusively, left the compartment.

The train was travelling across an artificially elevated ridge, and travelling hard, which scarcely made it the best possible place for him to take his leave, but he had no choice. He reckoned that he was about a half-hour from his destination, a town called Point Osborne and he really did not relish the prospect of arriving there at the same time as those two and in the dark.

He tossed his grip over the side and prepared to follow it, both hands on the guard-rail ready to jump, when the carriage door opened and closed quickly behind him and even as he turned, knowing they had followed him, a flying fist struck him on the jaw. His head jerked and he felt warm blood surge down the back of his throat. They seized his arms while he was still recovering from the blow and hit him again.

'You should've stayed where you was, Talbot,' one of them hissed in his ear and Talbot strained to revive himself.

'Gentleman doesn't want to ride all the way, Billy,' Castle spat. 'We ought to give him a refund on his ticket.'

Billy laughed abrasively, like a jackass and Talbot felt the ground lurch under him as they tilted him over the side of the guard-rail.

'Go back to your horse shit, Talbot. That's where you belong. You stay here and something pretty damned bad is gonna happen to you,' the voice sizzled down at him, flecked with spittle.

'Besides,' Castle finished, 'you-all won't like it at that Spanish place,

Talbot. I can promise you that.'

And a second later he was sent tumbling out into space. He turned in mid air and his heels raked into the ground as he hit the slope standing, toppled into a further somersault and landed this time on his back, felt his shirt rip on the jagged, stony ground as stones and grit bit into his flesh. A particularly rough stretch turned him again and as he twisted on to his face he was able to dig his hands into the dirt and hold on, slowing himself, wedging his feet into the loose gravel.

He stopped sliding eventually and the coarse alkaline dust settled on him, dredged his hair and was swept down his face in grey veins by a river of sweat from his brow.

For a time he had no will to move. He was hurting in too many places to count or care for. The train had long since hurtled into the distance and there was an unfriendly, desert-like silence on the land.

He stood up shakily, coughed and

spat up some dust and grit he had swallowed and dragged a ragged, dirty sleeve across his forehead. The sleeve came away bloody and he felt for the injury with trembling fingers. It was a broad, shallow cut, just inside the hairline. One knee had been knocked out of his pants and further, he could not find his hat, cast about for it dizzily, but had to turn away eventually without it, searching now for his grip. The further back he walked to find it, the stiffer his right knee became. By the time he reached the battered leather bag, he was limping badly.

He sat down here to inspect the damage and rolled back the leg of his pants, his eyes narrowing as he looked at the ugly, bleeding gash. He bound it up tightly with a clean handkerchief taken from his grip, rolled down his pants' leg and carefully stood up. The sun was nearly down amongst those far-off hills now, but not far enough down to stop beating like a club on his unprotected head as he climbed away from the tracks. He began searching for a piece of high ground from which to assess his situation and, seeing a grassy mound perhaps a quarter of a mile away, began limping towards it.

As he walked he reflected on his abrupt departure from the train. It seemed that they did not after all intend to kill him, not unless he took his half-share. And they had seemed confident that he would decide to leave once he saw the ranch, or the Spanish place, as they had called it. He wondered, as he massaged the hard swelling on his jaw, what they would do if he decided to stay.

He climbed his piece of high ground and looked slowly around him. The railway tracks wound continuously into the south and west, the hills lay directly to the west, and to the south, east and north lay a seemingly endless vista of grassland. Viewed from a distance it had the appearance of a huge crop of wheat, yellow and patchily green, flattening and waving under a breeze that Talbot could not feel. And at first he could see no sign of civilization at all and then, as he turned around again more slowly, he saw a trace of drifting smoke on the horizon to the north. He lifted his grip and aimed himself towards it.

3

It was not, he found, a house that he had seen from the distance, but a small town. Passed over by the railroad in favour of the more prosperous river town of Point Osborn, Caldwell had survived the railroad company's decision by still being the main way station for the north-south stage line.

Talbot walked along the main street, noting that it had a saloon, boarding house, general store, bank, grain merchant and a gunsmith but he did not avail himself of any of their merchandise, though most of the stores were still open for business. He had seen at the end of the street the blacksmith's workshop with corrals and livery barn adjoining, owned, the sign said, by J. Casey and Son. Maybe somebody there could give him directions and a horse so that he might ride directly to the

17

ranch. He walked inside the stable, since there seemed to be no one about outside and, by the light of a single lamp hung from the rafters, he witnessed a scene that chilled him.

The girl was nineteen, looked younger, had blonde, short cut, absolutely straight hair. She held a shotgun in her hands, as if it were a plaything, the stock cradled comfortably in the hollow of her thin shoulder, where the impact of the recoil would probably break a bone or two. She had in her grey eyes a look of awareness about her situation that was heightened by a smile on her face that was half a sneer.

'If you take just one step closer I'll shoot you in the knees.'

She addressed herself to the taller of the two men who were menacing her, a fellow called Baker, a big, rugged man with an ugly, prizefighter's face. Baker looked at his partner, Conrad, who stood parallel to him, about six feet away. Conrad was thinner than his friend, with a prominent Adam's apple and a shock of coarse, black hair. They were finding it hard to look intimidated by a little girl, although they did not underestimate the damage that the weapon would do if it went off.

'Put that gun down before you hurt yourself,' Baker warned her sternly.

The girl gave a short, low, husky laugh and shifted her stance a fraction.

'Would you like to know what my dad calls this piece?' she asked in a conversational tone. 'He says it's his rattlesnake gun.'

Conrad took a wary step backward, his eyes suddenly nervous.

'Let's leave it, Matt,' he cautioned.

'And even if I miss with it,' she continued calmly. 'The noise will bring the whole damn town.'

'Come on, Matt,' Conrad urged, half turning to go. Baker rocked slightly forward on the balls of his feet, as if to make a grab at her, but seemed to think better of it and with a grunt of frustration, turned to leave. It was an old trick and she fell for it, though her concentration slipped for only a second, perhaps with relief.

Baker whirled on her, grasping and jerking the gun barrels upwards. Her finger contracted instinctively and the explosion blasted a hole in the roof, showering them with splintered, powdered wood and straw.

They tussled briefly and the shotgun was wrenched out of her hands and flung aside. Conrad came around behind and lifted her in the air, his rough hands crushing her slight young breasts. She kicked him in the groin with a viciously back-swinging heel and jammed her elbow into his throat, then she scratched Baker, with short, ragged nails, gouging a furrow of angry, scarlet marks on both cheeks which incensed him beyond reason. He spread-eagled her on the ground, kneeling on her arms, ready to crush the resistance out of her with fists.

The shaft of the rake bore down from behind and hit him squarely across the back. He yelped and fell away, deaf to

20

that too-late shout of warning from Conrad. The newcomer tossed aside the shattered rake handle and went after Conrad while the girl scrambled to her feet out of Baker's way, for he was not down long and not out at all. Bellowing and cursing, he swung around, looking for the phantom who had brained him with the rake handle, nearly blinded by his own rage. He did not see the girl and for the moment she was safe, for Baker wanted Talbot.

Conrad had already taken two savage punches from the tall, dark-haired intruder, who had crowded him into a corner and, with blood flooding from a shattered upper lip, was trying to protect his face from further punishment, just as Baker came charging in behind the new man, ready to strike.

She shouted to warn Talbot of the danger but not quickly enough. The murderous kidney punch felled him. His face drained of all colour and he toppled and collapsed on the straw, but was down for a few seconds only, rolled and swayed to his feet again, planting his shoulders against a wall for support.

They began moving in on him, warily, cautious of those quick fists. But there was only a brief exchange of blows. The shots had achieved what the girl had predicted they would, for Caldwell was a peaceful place and gunshots were rare events. Baker and Conrad retreated to the back door as they heard the clamour outside of an approaching crowd.

'You made a bad mistake,' Baker growled over his shoulder at Talbot. 'You should've minded your nose. I'll see you another time.'

'Sure,' the girl jeered at his retreating back. 'Keep a piece of steak over both eyes and you might even see daylight tomorrow.'

The stable door was suddenly full of people and while the girl explained and showed them where her attackers had gone, Talbot melted quietly into the shadows and reached the street, staggering a little, one hand at his back. He made it as far as the trough and water pump in front of the stable and came to a halt there, leaning on the edge, close to passing out.

'This is the man, Max,' he heard a familiar, husky voice say and he raised his eyes as the girl came up to him. With her was a big good-looking, dark-haired man, with a genial face and intelligent dark-blue eyes.

'Want to thank you for what you did back there, friend. You saved our girl here from bein' abducted, maybe killed.'

The man, who spoke with a deep, slow, Tennessee accent, watched closely as Talbot cupped a little cold water and raised it to the freshly bleeding cut on his forehead.

''Course, she wouldn't have bin in any danger if she had done like I told her to and stayed at the feed store,' Max continued, turning now to the girl to give her the roasting he felt she deserved. 'What in the world got into you to go to the livery barn alone after I told you to stay put?'

'I'm not your little puppy, Max Ryan,' she railed at him, swinging around to defend herself, her grey eyes sparking with fury, 'following along at your heels when you say so.'

'Damn it, Trisa,' he leaned close to her, to contain his fury between the two of them, 'your pa would spit-roast me if anything was to happen to you, not to mention what Louise would do to me. Now I get to go home and tell them I had to trust your safety to a complete stranger, no offence meant to you, sir,' he said in an aside to Talbot.

'Well, if you would just stop lecturin' on at me for one second, I'll tell you why I left the feed store,' Trisa said and both men waited, Max still leaning towards her, Talbot slightly amused by the altercation.

'Somebody gave me a note that said you wanted me to go there,' she explained, and she dug into the back pocket of her pants to pull out the scrap of dirty paper, handing it to Max. It was not even an attempt at a forgery, written by someone who spelled the word livery as 'livri'. He looked at her incredulously and shook his head, stuffed the paper into his pocket and settled his hat on his head again as if that would help to calm him down.

'I beg your pardon,' he said, turning again to Talbot. 'My name's Ryan. Max Ryan,' he went on, holding out a friendly hand. Talbot straightened away from the distorted reflection of himself in the trough water and turned stiffly, accepting the hand.

'Talbot,' he said, taking a short, painful breath. 'Nathan Talbot.'

Ryan looked surprised and then laughed softly.

'Well, I'll be damned. We were wonderin' if you were ever gonna get here, weren't we, Trisa?'

The girl smiled but her eyes were concerned. She saw Talbot sway and put a hand to the pump for support. Max said, 'Mr Saville will be real glad to see you.'

Talbot stared at him and Max and the girl exchanged looks.

'Saville . . . ?' he said, sounding dazed.

'You were on your way to the Saville ranch, weren't you?'

'No. No Velarde ranch, I think it's called.'

'Well, we're both right,' Max laughed. 'It used to be called Velarde years ago, before the Saville family owned it. Sometimes people call it the Spanish ranch too. Can be confusing for strangers.'

Trisa smiled at Max's explanation but turned back to Talbot to enlarge on his introduction.

'I'm Trisa Saville. It's my dad that's bin waiting for you to come. You should've sent a wire or somethin' and we would've come get you.'

Talbot shifted his hold on the trough pump and stared at the girl with the grey eyes and something stuck a knell at his heart. It could not be. He gave a slow blink and took a step away, releasing his hold on the pump.

'Oh . . . damn,' he said softly and then he collapsed, senseless, into the road, before Max could catch him.

4

Three weeks of rain had reduced the riverside encampment to a swamp of inadequately anchored tents and wagons, the mud trampled and churned by boot heels and horse hoofs and wagon wheels into a morass, brownish-yellow and treacherous underfoot. Everything was wet, the canvas, the clothes of the men who patrolled the riverbank, the horses and gear, all sodden by a constant drizzle of fine rain that came unceasingly from an ugly, lowering sky.

Today was the first day it hadn't rained in weeks, Sergeant Lyons realized as he crossed the camp. Lyons was a big man, heavy in the shoulders and chest and crossing that half-submerged stretch of ground between the wooden bridge and the captain's tent was proving none too easy for him. He walked delicately, like a woman in

28

high-heeled shoes, not pressing his feet down too firmly into the stuff because then the slime clung stubbornly, dragging a man down till he was trapped in a bog of his own making.

But he completed his journey unscathed, save for being sprayed by the backlash from a struggling wagon and team and entered the bivouac cursing and rubbing the splatter marks from the front of his blouse. He dismissed the soldier who had been with the captain through the night, for in his delirium he was apt to try to throw himself off the cot. For three days and nights now Captain Talbot had been in the grip of a fever that had reduced the man to a sweating, delirious shadow, and in the absence of immediate medical aid, Lyons had personally been nursing him, dosing him with quinine.

Today he seemed less feverish, appeared to be in a genuine sleep. His face was colourless, lips chalky and dry, hair clamped in against his head and his chin darkened by a stubble that looked strange on a face that had always been close shaven, though it was fashionable, and in the field practical, to let beard and whiskers flourish.

His right hand lay on his chest and Lyons closed his fingers around the wrist to take a pulse. The beat was rather fast but the strength of it reassured the sergeant, as he sat down now on the stool by the cot-side. His touch had roused the captain. He turned his head and his eyes, slitting reluctantly against the light, were still glassy and bright.

'What is it, Sergeant?' he asked hoarsely.

'You know me, Captain?'

'What?' He looked alarmed for a moment until his sergeant grinned at him.

'You didn't know me yesterday.'

'Yesterday,' he sighed and let his head sink back on to the folded greatcoat that was his pillow.

'How you feelin' this mornin'?'

'Thirsty.'

Lyons took a bottle from his tunic. It

was only water but it was clean, from the spring in the little wood behind the camp, not from the muddy river, and Talbot was grateful for it and swallowed most of what was in the container, while Lyons supported him.

'How about some food?' the sergeant went on, encouraged. 'Could you try a bite to eat?'

The captain swallowed a sensation of sickness in his throat and turned his head weakly on the pillow.

'Not today, Lyons.'

He looked around at the man who had nursed him unswervingly these past days. Hazily, he was able to recall that last night was the first that Lyons had not spent at his bedside.

'You could use a shave, Sergeant.'

'I know,' Lyons said, scrubbing his nails against his chin. 'I'll give you a shave if you want.'

'Later maybe.'

'Rest first. Get some sleep. I'll keep the water hot.'

'I'll have to get up off this cot soon.'

31

'You get up right now and you'll fall down,' Lyons cautioned.

'Right. I know. Legs all gone to hell.'

'You've bin a mighty sick man, sir.'

Talbot was aware of it. The fever had been working on him for days, ever since their arrival at this godforsaken bridge, waiting for orders that never came, waiting for the entire Confederate army to appear on the other side of the bridge, waiting for the fever to get them all.

Except that this fever was not caused by the chill and the dampness of Cherry Bridge. He knew from the first shiver, the first dull headache behind his eyes, that it was the start of a bout of malaria, not his first, nor his last.

At first he had suffered nausea and dizziness and uncontrollable bouts of shaking, culminating in his collapse, in his own tent, thank God, where the men could not see their commanding officer convulsed with the shakes, drenched with cold and then burning sweat, being physically held down while

32

he raved and struggled.

'I suppose Lieutenant Saville is taking care of things in his usual fashion?' he asked quietly.

'Oh yes sir,' Lyons smiled. 'Lieutenant Saville is in total command.' They exchanged looks of mutual understanding. Saville was ambitious. He had been a lieutenant too long now and was itching for a chance to improve his lowly rank, at whatever cost. He was a hothead. The captain, before his illness, had spent a good deal of time pouring cold water on Lieutenant Howard Saville's rash ambitions, with a mixed degree of success.

'Maybe word will come for us to move today,' he said thoughtfully.

'If it does, we'll have the carrying of you out of here. You wouldn't want that, would you, sir?'

'I suppose not. Not until we've taken care of the damn bridge first. If I have to get carried away from here, it'll have to be with a southern bullet in me. Otherwise my mother would never be able to hold her head up in public.'

He spoke with heavy sarcasm, scornful of heroics and of his mother's longing for military glory, at her son's expense. Talbot rarely spoke of his family and, for Lyons, this was a rare glimpse of the captain's private side.

'Can't go on forever,' Lyons said softly. 'You'n me'll be on our way home soon and southern bullets be damned.'

The captain returned to contemplating the grey bivouac wall. He had felt sometimes during the last few nights that he had fought and won the entire war single-handed, had been thoroughly disappointed to wake and find that he was still here, still camped on a swamp.

'You should be an officer,' he said, turning his head around again to look at his large, dependable sergeant. 'Union needs your breed of men.'

Lyons was unruffled by the backhanded compliment, for though it was said in that same slightly mocking tone, Lyons knew that Talbot meant it, that he trusted and depended on his sergeant more than he did the plastic and shallow Howard Saville.

Those were to be Captain Talbot's last coherent words for some time, for without warning his face took on an ashen hue, beaded with cold sweat, the beginnings, Lyons knew, of a fit of the shakes.

'Oh God,' Talbot groaned, putting the back of his wrist to his mouth, just as his body began to quiver and vibrate uncontrollably. Lyons held him down, with a big hand on either shoulder, and stayed with him until it was over. It was a relatively short thrashing bout, shorter than any that had preceded it, but it left him just as weak and washed out as the others, wanting to vomit, with nothing left inside him worth bringing up. When it was finished, he hadn't the strength to speak, his eyes smoky with exhaustion.

'All right now, sir?' Lyons asked him anxiously, but the captain, with his cheek pressed to the bulky wool of his winter coat, had drifted into sleep. Lyons sank back on to the stool. He armed sweat from his face and released a long breath, then took another container from his pocket, a small, flat, metal flask that didn't hold water, and took a restorative pull of liquor from it.

'Union needs you too, sir,' he told the sleeping officer. 'What it don't need is that useless, arrogant bastard Saville in charge for much longer.'

5

Later that day Sergeant Lyons gave his report to a sour-faced Lieutenant Saville. Their dislike was mutual but Lyons disguised it better.

'How is he?' Saville asked carelessly, his head bent over a duty roster. There was little else to occupy his time in this forgotten backwater. If Talbot were not such an unambitious plodder, he thought harshly, they might be in a much handier position instead of a damned swamp.

'He's mending,' Lyons affirmed.

'Well, you ought to know,' Saville said, with a tight little smile that fitted narrowly on his handsome face. 'You've been nursing him constantly, I hear, like a faithful old watchdog.'

'Beg pardon, sir?' Lyons lifted an eyebrow, refusing to rise to the bait.

'Never mind. I want a report on his

condition this evening. If there's no improvement, I'm having him sent back to the supply lines.'

The sergeant poked his tongue into his cheek and shrugged. Not if he's awake to say different, he thought, but he merely saluted, and only he could make a salute seem insolent, and made his way back to the captain. As he cleared the entrance to Saville's quarters, he turned his head and hurled a mouthful of spit at the tent wall.

'Bastard,' he swore under his breath.

That evening, with difficulty in the cramped tent, he shaved the captain, helped him into a fresh shirt and coaxed him to eat a bite of hot food. Talbot was reading some letters, propped up with the folded coat at his back and looking a great deal better than he felt when Saville came for his report.

Obviously surprised by the shaven face and lack of fever, Saville inquired politely but coldly after his captain's health, noticing as he did the expression on Lyon's face, like a great, smug tomcat.

'Thanks to Sergeant Lyons I'm much improved, thank you, Lieutenant.'

The captain's civility was flawless, the product of his upbringing and background. His tone was even and his tired face expressionless. Sergeant Lyons saw really clearly tonight the difference between the two men. Talbot was a gentleman, and Saville resented it, resented his captain's natural courtesy, leadership skills and quiet competence, for Nathan Talbot was everything Saville could never be. He had come to the captain's bivouac tonight to exercise his authority and take command and now that he found he could not, he was at a loss.

'Was there something on your mind, Lieutenant?' Talbot asked.

'Well, sir,' Saville took the fateful plunge. 'I thought you might not be well enough . . . that is to say, if I had not found you so obviously rallying to Sergeant Lyon's efforts, I had it in mind . . . I had it in my mind, sir, to send you to the supply lines, to a field hospital, for some proper medical care.'

He bolted the last sentence recklessly, hoping that Talbot might agree, might admit that he belonged in a hospital. But the captain's face had stiffened with anger and Saville saw that he had made a crucial error.

'You had it in mind to do what?' he asked, his voice dangerously quiet.

'Sir, we have been without a commanding officer, and you have been ill, in fact are still far from — '

'I was ill. Tomorrow I will be making an inspection of this camp and you had better pray that it meets my expectations. As to what you had in your mind, if you had followed that foolish impulse, I would have had your rank and then your hide.'

'Surely — '

'No matter how sick I am, I stay here at my post. Unless I am dismembered or dead, I stay. And Mister Saville?' Talbot pushed himself up a little, 'You do not, you will never have the authority to send me anywhere.'

'Sir — '

'You're dismissed, Lieutenant.'

The colour fled and then unexpectedly flooded back to Howard Saville's face. He shot a murderous look at Lyons and then wheeled smartly out of the tent, the flush of hot colour in his face spreading to his neck. Emerging into the cool, damp evening air, he almost collided with Corporal Holden.

'Dispatch rider just came in, sir,' Holden said, offering an oilskin wrapped package.

'All right, I'll take it,' Saville barked, his anger with Talbot momentarily eclipsed by the sight of those dispatches, which probably meant they'd be moving from this godforsaken bridge.

'There's a doctor here too, sir. A Major Jerome.'

Saville looked up in surprise from the package in his hand. The doctor had served with them last year, and it was the same Doctor Jerome who moved into the small circle of light cast by the lantern in Talbot's quarters, a dark-haired, sallow-complexioned, thoughtful-looking, slenderish man in his early thirties.

'Good to see you again, Doctor,' Saville said neutrally.

'Lieutenant.'

'You've come just in time, sir. The captain's been fevered for some days. I have been trying to persuade him to return to the supply lines for medical aid, but without success.'

Jerome tilted his head and smiled kindly at Saville, not surprised to find the young lieutenant still chafing against his steady, unambitious captain, against everything and everybody who opposed him.

'You won't get Nathan Talbot to go anywhere he doesn't want to go, son. Better men before you have tried and failed. Is he in here?'

Saville nodded. He had forgotten that Jerome and Talbot were close friends, friends before the war. If he had expected an ally, he was mistaken.

'Good night then, sir.' He saluted

and turned towards his own quarters, the dispatches forgotten, still in his hand.

Jerome lowered his head and ducked into the tent, saw Sergeant Lyons first and smiled at him. Lyons grinned back at him, relieved to see those surgeon's tabs on Jerome's shoulders, saluted first, then heartily shook the doctor's hand.

'Well, for God's sake. You don't know how glad I am to see you, Doc.'

'How are you, Sergeant?'

'Oh, I'm all right,' Lyons said, with a meaningful nod over his shoulder to the man on the cot. Jerome gave a little nod of understanding.

'Will you see to it my horse is taken care of, Sergeant, and bring my bag in here?'

'Right away, sir.'

Talbot, his face flushed with pleasure, raised himself, his hand outstretched.

'David. What in the world are you doing here?'

'Hello, Nathan. How are you?' He

took the hand and held it in both of his.

'I've been ill. Fine now.'

Doctor Jerome removed his wet outer garments and came around the side of the cot. He sat down to take a closer look, deep concern in his eyes.

'You've been ill all right. Bad bout this time huh?'

'Bad enough,' Talbot admitted, leaning back on his makeshift pillow. 'The sergeant has been taking good care of me. I just now nipped a little scheme of Saville's in the bud. He wanted to send me off to a field hospital.'

'Yes, he was ever thoughtful,' Jerome smiled. 'But whatever his motives, he is right, you know. You need rest and care after one of these bouts, not wet quarters and camp food.'

'We're expecting our marching orders any day now. I have to be on my feet when they come,' Talbot said emphatically. Jerome looked at him in alarm. He had heard this kind of talk before. The sergeant returned with his surgical case and Jerome opened it and began examining Talbot, deftly unbuttoning the front of his blouse to listen to heart and lungs, peering into eyes, depressing fingernails, tenderly pressing glands in the throat, armpit and groin. He took his time, with an abstracted thoroughness, his face giving nothing away.

'You're over the worst, but not ready for getting up yet. Not by a long chalk,' he finally pronounced. Even the simple examination had tired Talbot. As he struggled to re-button his shirt, Jerome quietly watched him.

'Well, my friend, we're both a long way from Boston,' the doctor observed. 'I wonder if your mother is still holding her Friday night socials.'

'Why should she not?' Talbot asked drily. 'The slight inconvenience of Civil War will not affect her one way or another.'

Jerome knew Talbot's mother well. He gave a little nod of agreement.

'What have they sent you here for, David? I didn't get any word you were coming.'

'I don't know. I came with a dispatch rider, so I suppose the answer will be in that packet Saville has.'

'Dispatches?'

'Maybe those marching orders you spoke of.'

'Sergeant?'

Lyons poked his head around the corner of the tent flap.

'Sir?'

'Lieutenant Saville has dispatches the doctor just brought in. I want to see them.'

'Now, sir?'

'Yesterday, Sergeant.'

'Right away, sir.'

'I'll leave you to it, Nathan. I guess I'll go see if I can find a bite of supper and a place to sleep.'

'Glad to have you along, David.'

Jerome smiled and closed his surgical case with a little snap.

'We'll see how glad you are in the morning, when I pull rank and stop you from getting up too soon. Goodnight, Nathan.'

6

Sergeant Lyons found him in the morning, struggling to pull on his boots, his face white with exertion.

'Here now,' Lyons admonished him. 'Where do you think you're goin'?'

'Help me with this damned boot,' Talbot swore.

'Sir, I don't think — '

'I have to get up, Sergeant, whether we both like it or not. We're pulling stakes tonight.'

Lyons sighed mightily but stooped and effortlessly drew the boot on for him. His round, ruddy face spoke volumes.

'You're not fit yet.'

'I know, Sergeant,' Talbot admitted. 'But we both know that those orders that came in last night mean an end to my convalescence.'

Sergeant Lyons shook his head

gravely, watching as little spots of high colour began to appear on the captain's cheeks, stark in contrast to the ashen hue of the rest of his face.

'Seems to me anyway that Doc Jerome will have the last word.'

'Have the last word on what?' said Jerome from the door.

'He wants to get up, Doc,' Lyons said sternly and they both looked down at him.

'You're not serious?' Jerome frowned and threw a look at Lyons.

'Sergeant, has Lieutenant Saville begun work on the bridge?' Talbot asked, ignoring the doctor.

'Yes, sir, they started at dawn like you wanted.'

'Good. We've got to be ready to blow the bridge in twelve hours.'

'Then it'll have to be blown without you, Nathan,' Jerome informed him with quiet conviction.

'Excuse me, Doctor, I have to inspect the camp now. Sergeant, have my horse brought round if you would.'

Seeing the hopelessness of further argument, Lyons gave a shrug and left.

'Nathan, you have to turn command over to Saville,' Jerome said and Talbot gave him a pained look.

'Now you're not being serious.'

Talbot stood up, carefully, and walked slowly but unaided out into the daylight he had not seen for almost a week, to where Lyons stood with his horse. The sergeant gave him a leg up and then stood back with arms folded, by the doctor's side, to watch with critical eye. Talbot clutched at the reins, feeling dizzy and nauseous.

'What's wrong,' Jerome asked him and he sounded to Talbot as if he were at the other end of a long tunnel. He shook his head impatiently and touched a light heel to the chestnut's flanks, staunchly ignored the fact that the ground seemed a good quarter of a mile down and began making an inspection of the camp.

He rode continuously towards the wooden bridge which they had ostensibly been guarding a little too long for comfort and safety and which, tonight, they would blow to kindling. The orders which Saville had finally handed over last night had explained why they had been camped by Cherry Bridge for so long, miles away from any fighting.

They had been sent here three weeks ago, a mixture of infantry and some of Captain Morton's engineers. Talbot had been hand-picked for the task by Crittenden, although they were under direct orders from the chief of scouts, John Noble, to guard Cherry Bridge and when the time was right, to assist a scouting party who were on the other side of the river, deep behind enemy lines. It had been intended that Talbot's party would be there for no more than three days. And then the rains came, three weeks of it and everything had ground to a halt. Even some of the trains had stopped running, when track and bridges had been washed away. The entire army of the Cumberland was stopped in its tracks. But now the weather had cleared and the orders had come for them to complete their mission.

The scouting party that had been sent across the river more than a month ago had been given three tasks and had been told to carry them out or keep travelling and take up residence in Mexico. On paper their remit looked impossible. In reality, they had managed to complete two of their tasks. They had gathered sensitive information from two Union spies and they had rescued a captured Union officer who had yet further information needed by the generals. Their last assignment was to blow up a hidden arsenal, nothing very large or very important but in war little things added up sometimes to victory.

That third commission, the destruction of the weapons' store, was to take place tonight. Once done, they would have to get out quickly and the quickest way back was over Cherry Bridge. Talbot had orders to get those men back over the bridge and then destroy it, to ensure they could not be followed. It was of the utmost importance that those men should return safely to the north with everything they knew.

And he would have to send a small party over the bridge to escort the raiding party back. Apparently they had run into a little trouble and there were injuries. Despite what he had said to Jerome, he knew he would have to turn that duty over to Saville. He could scarcely ride a circuit of his own camp, let alone lead a scouting party.

The men of his company turned to watch him and to a man they saluted or called out to him, asking after his health, then turned away to look at one another, shaking their heads. He was worn fine by his illness and understood their looks. He knew he scarcely inspired confidence.

At the bridge, he sat for a minute watching the engineers preparing it for destruction. As they swarmed over the stout timber structure with powder kegs and fuse wire, their operations were supervised by Saville, barking out his commands with an impatient, hectoring tone, dispensing liberal doses of sarcasm, threatening punishment or violence where neither was merited, deriding the men regardless of the speed or quality of their work. His simple maxim was that the common soldier was no better than a jackass, stupid, lazy and stubborn.

Talbot watched him with a familiar feeling of dismay and irritation, wishing his young officer's energy and undoubted intelligence could be channelled to some better effect than making everyone's life a misery.

As if sensing his captain's thoughts, Saville turned in time to see Talbot dismount, awkwardly, his knees refusing to give that necessary little bit as his feet touched ground. Jarred by his abrupt landing, he staggered, but a quick hand caught his elbow, steadying him.

'All right, sir?' It was a young corporal called Roberts, a soldier who liked to make himself agreeable to anybody above him in rank. He spent altogether too much time in Saville's company for Talbot's liking and shared the lieutenant's unpleasant views on discipline.

'How is the work going?'

'We're nearly through now, sir.'

He walked to the river bank and watched as they finished threading the last length of fuse wire up along the parapet, ready for the match that would plunge the whole structure into the dangerously swollen, surging river.

'What's the plan, sir?' Saville asked, appearing suddenly at his right side. 'Are you going across with the relief party?'

Despite the outwardly respectful tone, Talbot detected the sneer in Saville's voice but as usual, masked his dislike of the man.

'No, Lieutenant, I won't be going with the relief party. Pick your men, about a dozen all told, I think, and leave as soon as it's dark.'

'Very good, sir.'

'And Saville, don't foul it up,' Talbot told him, gently and quietly, so that no one else would hear. 'Or I'll break you and your little schemes to further your career like a dry stick.'

Saville glanced furtively over his shoulder at the other men, at Roberts, who was nearest and then back at Talbot, his youthful face, still boyish, still a little downy, turning blotchy with anger.

'I'll try not to let you down, sir,' he said, shutting his back teeth on what he really wanted to say. Talbot nodded wearily and returned to his horse.

'Let me give you a boost, sir,' Roberts offered helpfully. The captain put his foot into the basket Roberts made of his hands and stepped up, experiencing the same sick giddiness as before. Saville watched him, absently winding a length of cord around his fingers, smiling faintly.

Returning to his bivouac, Talbot found Lyons and Jerome both standing in the same spot, as if they'd never moved. They exchanged looks as he brought the big horse around in front of them.

'Seen all you want?' Jerome asked him tersely. Talbot slipped to the ground without answering, holding on to the pommel for support.

'You look like hell. I want you to go in that tent and lie down like I told you,' Jerome ordered and Talbot gave a little nod of collapsed resistance and, taking his hands from the pommel, began to fall. Lyons and Jerome both quickly caught him between them and carried him inside.

7

Saville and his twelve men had been gone for two hours when it suddenly occurred to Talbot that thirteen men had crossed the bridge. Unlucky. He shivered, but that was only river-damp, not superstition. He and Lyons and Jerome were stationed on the bridge-head, waiting and listening.

The doctor and Sergeant Lyons had laced their mugs of hot coffee with some of the doctor's very good French brandy, but Talbot was denied any liquor in his cup. Malaria and brandy, the doctor reminded him, were a bad mix. Talbot didn't argue or even drink the hot coffee. Nothing could warm the deep and penetrating chill in his bones and blood, the dredging cold that came from illness, from the imminent relapse that the doctor had warned him was inevitable.

He had already had the last word with the doctor. When everyone was safely across, he would remain behind to blow the bridge. He would not trust the task to anyone else, and nothing the doctor could say would persuade him otherwise. All he had to do after all was put a match to the covered fuse when the first horse hoofs struck that bridge, then take cover till it blew. The fuse was a long one, five minutes, Howard had said, more than enough time for everyone to get clear.

He took out his own half-hunter and stared at it without properly seeing the time, his vision blurring and then clearing as he blinked several times. Almost three hours had elapsed since the relief party had left. He turned and looked at the already depleted camp-site, everything packed up ready to move.

'They're coming,' Lyons said a little more loudly than he intended and Talbot took one or two steps on to the bridge, listening. He could hear horses, but not many, maybe no more than a dozen. There were ten; six from the original raiding party of eighteen and four from Saville's thirteen.

They came across the bridge slowly and Talbot saw that nearly all of the original six looked as tired and done in as he did. They barely raised their heads to salute him as they trooped by. Corporal Holden, bringing up the rear, sprang from his horse to give his report.

'Lieutenant Saville should be here in about another hour, sir. He stayed to help them blow up that arsenal. Well, it wasn't hardly what you would call an arsenal, just an old cabin and only two young fellas left to guard her.'

'Did you take them prisoner, Corporal? Did you bring them back with you?'

'No, sir,' Holden said slowly, shaking his head. 'They put up a pretty good fight, sir. They're both dead.'

'All right Holden. What about the prisoner, the officer they were going to try to bring out?'

'He passed you a minute ago, sir. He's wounded pretty bad.'

'Well done, Corporal. You've done a fine job.'

'Sir, thank you, sir.' Holden flexed his shoulders back with pride at Talbot's praise. After three hours of listening to Saville's curses and fault-finding it was a relief to be back in civilized company.

'Go on now, get everybody out of here. Help the sergeant.'

They put the wounded officer into one of the wagons and David Jerome, his reason for being sent to Cherry Bridge now made clear to him, got into the wagon with him, to try to make sure he survived the journey that lay ahead. He spoke to Talbot one last time.

'Come with us, Nathan. Leave the bridge to Lyons,' he asked for the tenth time.

'I'll be all right, David. I'll see you soon. Take care of him,' he nodded to the exhausted-looking soldier, who lay with closed eyes, his shoulder and upper arm heavily bandaged. He shook the doctor's hand and then watched him drive away. The sergeant didn't bother trying to persuade him. He simply brought Talbot's coat and roughly made him put it on, then put a fresh, hot coffee and brandy on the bridge parapet.

'Goodbye, sir.'

'Get them back safe, Sergeant. I'll see you in a little while.'

Talbot was finally alone, standing by the water, experiencing the unpleasant sensation of the cold river bank rising through his boots. An unfortunate moment to discover that he had a hole in the sole of one of them. He tilted the cup to his lips to drink the coffee and brandy and heard his teeth rattle against the rim.

The horizon remained dark. Talbot watched it steadfastly, when at last the sky lit up with a barrage of colour, followed half a beat later by a closely grouped series of explosions. Talbot watched the vivid red and orange sky, his own face reflecting the lurid bath of colour for a few seconds.

'All right,' he said softly. He watched the dramatically underlit clouds for another ten minutes before he heard the riders approach on the other side of the bridge. He knelt to the fuse box and waited, his own breathing sounding strangely loud in his ears, waiting and listening for the signal.

When it came, three shots fired in rapid succession, he lit the fuse and straightened just as the first horse hoofs struck the wooden bridge. He watched for only a second or two as the men began to cross the bridge, two abreast, no more than dark shapes in the night, with the occasional glint of reflected light on a spur or buckle, then he turned his back on them and began walking quickly to where his horse was tethered, fifty yards away, by the tree line.

Five minutes Saville had said. Not ten seconds later Talbot heard and then felt the explosion, felt it as a powerful body blow that rammed him face down into the ground and then relentlessly lifted and rolled him like a helpless rag doll. His back hit the ground and raw pain arced up and down his spine like a whipsaw.

Before he passed out, before the heat and the blinding brightness of the explosion died out in his brain, he heard them screaming, horses and men, heard them die and knew, in a split second of total, horrifying awareness, that he had killed them.

8

It was always the sensation of striking the ground that made him wake. His body gave a lurch and he gasped, throwing up his arms to protect himself from falling debris. There was no debris to fall on him. The room was dark and he was alone in it, lying on a large, unfamiliar, though comfortable bed.

His body relaxed a little and he lowered his arms. The dream always left a lingering sensation of anxiety which usually passed in a few minutes, but not tonight. Tonight Cherry Bridge had finally caught him up.

He started to climb out of the bed but a reeling dizziness left him clutching at the bedside table and he sank back down, fighting nausea, arms resting on his thighs, head down. From there he took a long, hard look at his situation.

A ruse, neither subtle nor very clever, had brought him here with depressing ease. He had been too preoccupied with Castle and Billy, though now it seemed that they too had been part of the ruse. It was ironic that after years of expecting something of the kind, waiting for somebody to come tracking him down who had lost kin on that bridge, who had lost something much more deeply personal than half a platoon, he should walk into a trap laid for him by a man who had not even bothered to stalk him, had done nothing more energetic than write a letter or two.

He stood up shakily and walked to the handsome pine dresser opposite the bed. In the mirror atop the dresser he regarded his reflection. His appearance depressed him so thoroughly that even as he looked at himself he saw his brown eyes tighten and narrow with distaste for this dishevelled stranger.

He stripped out of the torn, filthy clothing and washed in the jug of still warm water someone had thoughtfully provided. From his grip, which had been placed on a pine storage chest at the foot of the bed, he took fresh clothes and began to dress, with a slowness that maddened him, struggling with buttonholes and belt buckle and at the end of it desperately tired. He threw his dirty clothes into the bag and closed it, then let himself out quietly on to the corridor. From here a flight of stairs led down to the front door. He went down them slowly and carefully, anxious not to make a sound.

Max, when he had put Talbot to bed upstairs, went down to the kitchen in search of food. There were three people already there, who turned with expectant faces when Max walked into the room. Trisa, her father Gregory Saville, who sat in a wheelchair, and the Saville housekeeper, Louise.

'Is he all right?' Trisa asked him.

'He's asleep right now. Know better in the morning.'

He sat at the big, scrubbed, pine

table where the family always breakfasted and looked expectantly at Louise.

'I suppose you're hungry,' she stated, smiling.

'I didn't get any supper,' he complained. Louise hefted down the big fry pan and began to cook some bacon.

'Young lady, I think you've had enough excitement for one day. Time for bed I think,' Saville said to his daughter, who came and perched on the arm of his chair, her hand resting on his shoulder.

'I'll go to bed in a minute, Daddy. I was just waiting for Max to tell us if he was all right.'

'Think we should get the doctor for him, Max?'

'He's OK,' Max assured everyone. 'When he wakes up he'll have a head on him most likely. Anyway, Doc's out of town for a couple of weeks, remember.'

'He must have taken an unholy beating,' Saville said thoughtfully, accepting the cup of coffee Louise poured for him. He had seen his new half-partner carried into his house bloody and insensible, a victim already of the misfortunes that seemed to dog everyone who had dealings with the ranch.

'He didn't take it all from those two in the barn.'

'What do you mean, Max?'

'I mean he was mightily bruised for a man who'd been in a five-minute fist fight.' He added nothing further, but looked up from his plate of bacon and eggs and found Saville giving him a thoughtful look.

'Well,' Saville sighed, with a loving glance at Trisa, whose life had been returned to him intact tonight, thanks to Nathan Talbot. 'He's here now. We can get things settled.'

In the slight silence that ensued, they all heard the outer door quietly closing. With a little frown of surprise, Max got to his feet. He walked out to the hallway and opened the front door, looked out and saw a figure limping towards the corrals, carrying a leather grip.

'Hey, Nathan,' he called out, starting down the shallow steps in front of the house after him. 'Where you going?'

Talbot turned in alarm, lowering the grip to his feet. He stared at the foreman and braced himself for trouble.

'You should be in bed, Nathan. Come on in the house now,' he said as he reached for one of Talbot's arms to guide him back. Talbot put his own hand on Max's wrist to free himself, but even as he applied pressure, he felt his strength slip mysteriously away, felt the blood leave his face and he folded. Max put an arm around his waist.

'Easy now. Let's get you inside.'

He was led back into the house, his bag was left in the hallway and in the kitchen, where Max brought him, he found himself the object of intense interest and in at least one pair of eyes, hostile scrutiny. Talbot regarded the silent faces with dismay and made no protest when Max pushed a chair behind him and pressed him down on to it. A woman, fair-haired, kindly looking, perhaps thirty or a little younger came forward and poured a cup of coffee for him, laying her hand on his shoulder and looking into his face with motherly concern.

'Are you all right?'

'Thank you, yes,' he replied, looking up into her faded blue eyes.

'This is Louise,' Max introduced them. 'She takes care of everybody. And I guess you remember Trisa.'

Talbot looked at her again, noting with a touch of relief that there was very little of Howard in that face, those grey woman's eyes. The girl gave him the same concerned look that he remembered from the trough pump.

At length, somewhat unwillingly, he brought himself to look at the head of the house. Gregory Saville was a sick man but despite the burden of ill-health and recent worry, he was still a formidable looking individual. The head was held at an autocratic angle, the jaw arrogant. His hair, once fair, now almost white, was thick and luxuriant and wavy as Howard's had been, while his beard, moustache and eyebrows were very dark, a striking, handsome contrast. He resembled Howard far too much for Talbot's comfort, except for the eyes, which were the same grey as his daughter's, and gimlet sharp, missing nothing. The wheelchair he sat in was simply a small armchair that had been modified with a set of wheels and a lever brake, home-made but comfortable looking. And invalid or not, he gave Talbot a swift, sizing, summing look from those fierce eyes, a look that left him in no doubt about what Saville knew and thought about him, a look that stung, as it was meant to.

'How are you, sir?' Talbot said politely.

'I am as you see me,' Saville said abruptly. He did not offer to shake hands until Trisa suddenly wheeled him forward and he was forced to coldly give his right hand to an equally reluctant Talbot.

As Louise turned back to her stove,

she nudged Max with her hip and frowned. Max nodded. He had seen it too, the coolness on Saville's part towards Talbot and Talbot's forced return. They disliked one another and Max found himself absorbed, simply watching and listening, trying to figure out why.

'We all thank you for helping Trisa tonight,' Saville went on, offering his thanks with a flat smile of gratitude that masked his true feelings, but it was as false as his handshake. He did not want to owe Nathan Talbot any obligation and Talbot certainly did not want to be owed.

'I was in the right place at the right time, that's all. But now that I am here, I should tell you that I only came to wind up Lyle's business affairs. I don't know anything about ranching. I . . . have no interest in ranching.'

A curiously intense silence fell over the group and he felt that even Saville was not pleased by this little speech.

'The terms of Lyle's will state that

unless his successor takes a hand in the running of the ranch, he must sell his half back to me,' Saville said flatly. Talbot lifted his eyebrows, and gave a slight shrug. He had not wanted the half-share to begin with. Losing it would cost him nothing.

'I believe Lyle intended just exactly that transaction to take place. I think perhaps he wanted you to have your ranch restored to you as sole owner and in return I would have a small bequest. I expect you'd be happy to take over my share, sir.'

Again there was silence.

'Under normal circumstances I'd be more than glad to have my ranch restored to me but . . . at the moment, circumstances are not normal. There have been — ' Saville halted, looking cornered, reluctant to share the troubles they had all endured with this stranger. He fought an internal battle with himself before giving a decisive nod to no one in particular.

'Perhaps you would give me a few

moments of your time?' he asked, in that same cold, flat voice he had adopted with Talbot from the beginning, and which so perplexed the others, used to a warm, gentle, teasingly friendly head of the household. Max, obeying Saville's tilt of the chin, wheeled him out of the kitchen and crossed the hallway, to the room they called the library and Talbot, after a moment of hesitation, limped along after them.

He found himself in a long, low-ceilinged room, one wall of which was lined with shelves of books, most of them related to cattle rearing and animal husbandry of one sort or another and one or two calf-bound volumes in Spanish, left by some long ago Franciscan priest and contributing to the general Spanish feel of the house, with its cool plaster and tiles, built for the heat.

The room was carpeted with bright, woven rugs, the same that he had seen in the bedroom and hallway. Two long windows faced out on to the front yard and a stout oak desk took up the space immediately in front of them.

Max wheeled Saville in behind the desk and then with a hesitant look at Talbot, who had not been invited to sit in the beautifully carved visitor's chair on the other side of the desk, he left the two men alone.

Talbot, still letting his gaze rove around the handsome room, found himself looking suddenly at a photograph of Howard, which had been taken the year before Cherry Bridge. The man had taken pictures of nearly everyone, Jerome, Lyons, himself and apparently, Howard. Talbot had given his tin type to Jerome, asking him to send it back to his family for him. And Howard had sent his back to his folks.

It was an excellent likeness. In full dress uniform, hat under arm, proud and arrogant, hard-eyed, perfectly moulded head and face. He turned from it and Saville saw him shutter off whatever personal agony he had been reviewing then, his face becoming perfectly blank.

'So,' Saville said at last. 'You're the man who killed my son.'

Talbot made no reply, for what could he say?

'You must be proud of yourself, to kill a boy in cold blood. Howard wrote to me how you hated him and tried to kill his promotions. But I thought it was just professional jealousy. I never thought my son would die as a result of his commanding officer's malice.'

'What is it you want from me?' Talbot said to cut off Saville's inaccurate and prejudiced view of the way things had stood at Cherry Bridge. He shifted his weight from one foot to the other to ease the ache in his injured knee.

'You killed nigh on to a dozen men, innocent boys, mine amongst them. Howard would be here now but for you, here to help during these troubled times of ours. What price do you think I should claim for what you've taken away?'

'All these years I've been waiting for

someone to ask me the price,' Talbot said softly, almost to himself. 'I always assumed it would be a life for a life.'

'Well you assumed wrong.'

'But your men already tried to kill me tonight, when I was on the train.'

Saville gave his head an abrupt shake. He reached for a decanter on the corner of the desk and poured himself a small measure of the brandy in the decanter without offering his guest anything.

'I didn't send anyone to get you on the train. Looks like someone else wants your blood first. No. Not me. I've other plans for you, Captain Talbot.'

He turned the picture of his son around and looked at it thoughtfully.

'A few years before the start of the war I ran into financial difficulties, didn't know what to do, where to turn. Then I decided to advertise for a partner, someone who could put a little money into the ranch in return for a small profit, someone who wouldn't interfere with the day-to-day running of the place. James Lyle took up the partnership and bought a half-share. We never met, but we corresponded and I came to like and admire him.'

Saville turned the photograph back to its original place on the desk, the handsome, blond head turned so that it seemed to be looking directly at Talbot.

'When I found that he had died and left his half-share to you, and when I found out who you were, I did want to kill you. I wanted to kill you with my bare hands,' he said savagely, inclining forward in his chair as if that might still be an option. 'But then I was attacked, badly injured, left as you see me. And revenge is a luxury I can no longer afford. I need you to run this ranch until I am well again.'

'And I've already told you,' Talbot said wearily, 'I don't know anything about ranching.'

'I know a little bit about you, Captain. James Lyle told me about your father's shipping and freighting interests. He taught you everything about his business before he died, fully expecting you to step into his shoes. Because that's what sons generally do, isn't it?' Saville said with some bitterness. 'And that is what I mostly need at the moment, someone who can deal with the paperwork, balance the books, keep everything ticking over. I haven't the strength to stay in this chair for more than an hour at a time at the moment and the doctor doesn't even want me to be there that long. You have that knowledge and skill, I know. I also need someone to oversee the ranch work proper. At the moment Max is doing the work of three ranch hands. His own work is suffering. He needs help. Trisa does what she can but she already helps Louise and the two Mexican girls who do all the laundry and cooking for the hands. She works harder than anybody. You're a pretty poor bargain but I'm desperate. You're all I've got.'

'You seem sure I'll stay.'

'You're a man of honour aren't you,'

Saville spat. 'I know that deep down in that New England, puritan soul of yours you want to pay for your folly. Well here's your chance.'

'I was warned that I'd be dealt with if I stayed.' Talbot persisted, wondering how much more it would take to cause the throbbing veins in Saville's forehead to implode.

'I know your type, Captain. You value your hide too much to let yourself get killed. You're a survivor. I spotted you for one the minute I saw you. You'll stay. Max will show you what needs to be done, and teach you what you don't already know,' Saville said remorselessly and, examining Talbot's face, saw that he was already resigned to it.

'You've thought of everything.'

'I've got no choice. I don't want you here in my home. I hate you just for being alive when my son is in pieces somewhere, butchered by you. But the fact is I can't afford to buy you out right now. So in the meantime you stay, you learn and you stay alive.'

And so Talbot returned to the room he had awakened in and into which someone had thoughtfully returned his bag. He was sitting on the edge of the bed, wondering where to find the energy to remove his boots when Max knocked and looked in.

'Come on in,' Talbot said, stretching himself out on the big bed. Max wandered into the room and stood over Talbot, his hands jammed into his pockets, his broad good-looking face betraying none of his thoughts.

'You near passed out again, out there in the yard,' he said with a nod towards the window.

'I'm all right now,' Talbot said without conviction. He tried to flex his right knee and found that he could not, could feel that it was swollen and stiff. Talbot saw Max look at it, saw him think whatever private thought he had about it and say nothing. Talbot decided that he liked the Saville foreman.

'I can see you wondering about me, Max.'

'Man can do all the wondering he wants, can't he.'

'I jumped the train. That's how I hurt my knee.'

'You must've had a pretty powerful reason for doing a damn fool thing like that.'

'I had two reasons. Both of them were trying to persuade me not to come here.'

Max swore under his breath.

'Well, you didn't act like you were running off tonight when you helped Trisa. I don't think you scare that easy.'

'Would help some if I knew what was going on. Seems you've been having a little run of bad luck lately.'

'You might say,' Max smiled drily. 'We've had everything but the boils and frogs. We've got drought, we've had fire and accidents and polluted waterholes and men quittin' on us. There's a three-man workload for everybody, including Trisa, and I think the old man is a little short of cash. You didn't seem to hit it off right away; but he's a good man to work for. You won't regret staying unless those two on the train already made your mind up for you?' Max said, a pointed reminder of the fact that Talbot had tried to leave earlier tonight.

The last was meant as a goad to Talbot's masculine pride. What man ever backed down from an accusation of cowardice, no matter how thinly veiled, without a show of bravado. Talbot gave a short, bitter laugh.

'Mr Saville already convinced me that it would be in my own best interests to stay, Max. Maybe tomorrow you might show me around?'

'I'd be honoured and glad to, Nathan,' Max grinned and he bent down and pulled off Talbot's boots for him.

9

He was still wide awake when dawn began to draw unfamiliar patterns on the walls of the bedroom, and since he could hear the muted sounds of activity, doors opening and closing, crockery clinking, he went downstairs to begin his new career as manager of the Saville ranch. Pale and limping, feeling cornered and hating all of it, he arrived at the kitchen door. The others were all here, Max and Louise and Trisa, all but Saville, who had also had a bad night. The smell of hot bacon and eggs frying almost turned him back but Louise got her eye on him and led him in.

'You look like you spent the night in a hard chair,' she observed.

'Come and sit down here beside me,' Trisa invited and as he sat, a cup of steaming hot coffee was placed before him in a serviceable but still very good quality blue china cup and saucer. He took a few tentative sips and decided that Louise's coffee was almost worth staying for.

'What can I fix you? Eggs, pancakes?' she asked him.

'Nothing thanks. This is fine. I never eat much in the morning.'

Louise shook her head gravely, put her own plate down and sat to eat.

'I can see I'm going to have to take charge of you,' she promised and smiling a little, Talbot helped himself to another cup of coffee.

'I'm going into town today, Nathan,' Trisa began. 'Is there anything I can get you?'

'Is anyone going with you?' he asked, glancing at Max.

'I'm sending a couple of boys along.'

'Well, I lost my hat yesterday,' he smiled at Trisa. She stared at him for a second, as if she hadn't understood what he said and then she blinked and gave her head a little shake.

'I'll pick one out for you.'

'Trisa, you know you can't buy somebody else a hat,' Max said disparagingly.

'Well, his head can't be any bigger than yours,' she came back as quick and fresh with Max as she had been with her attackers in the barn. 'And I know your size.'

'Now don't you two start while I'm eating,' Louise warned with a smile at Talbot.

'I've got a spare you can use, Nathan. You'll need it this morning,' Max offered.

'I'll bring you a new one just the same,' Trisa insisted. 'Does this mean you're staying?'

He looked at Max, who stopped eating long enough to wait for his answer and he nodded.

'For a while, till your father is up and about again.'

Max gave a little nod of satisfaction. He didn't really understand why but it seemed important somehow that Talbot should stay and Trisa grinned, slapped the remains of her breakfast between two thick slices of bread and headed for the door as one of the hands looked around to call for her.

'See you later,' she called back cheerfully.

'I swear that girl has more energy than a stampede,' Louise laughed as she poured herself a cup of coffee, adding sugar and cream to hers.

'And she's very nearly as noisy as one,' said Max, reaching for another biscuit and two more slices of bacon.

'I can't think of anyone who could have faced up to those two the way she did last night, let alone a young girl,' Talbot said quietly and the others fell silent, thinking what would it be like without Trisa to keep them all in their place, to cheer everybody up when they were blue, to make more noise than a houseful. It hardly bore contemplating.

'When you're finished,' Max said, rising, 'I'll show you around the place.'

After the guided tour, Talbot, who

professed to know nothing of ranching, knew nevertheless that this was a fine ranch.

The house and outbuildings were of robust construction, clearly the work of skilled workmen, built to last, with little architectural touches that lifted the buildings out of the workaday. They were also laid out like a fort, as thoroughly protected as any military outpost, the main house standing on a slight elevation. It was a long, white, two storeyed structure, with a pink, tiled roof and a spacious covered veranda at the front, a beautiful colonnaded walk that was an oasis of liquid cool in the building heat. It was Spanish in design and construction, a home fit for a cattle baron. Talbot at least understood Saville's strong sense of property when he looked at such a house. The whole place had the appearance of prosperity and yet Talbot felt an undercurrent. Introduced to one or two of the hands, he picked up on their hostility. Everybody it seemed was an enemy until proven otherwise. When he had seen all there was to see here, he and Max rode out together to take a look at the rest of the property.

Talbot was glad of Max's broad-brimmed black hat for the sun stabbed fiercely against his face, trying to find his eyes under its protective shade. The heat, as they rode, struck down with a violence he found exhausting, the hard glare of sunlight murdering his eyes, sometimes killing the power of the retina to distinguish colour.

They rode about all day, examining the low state of most of the waterholes, looking at red cattle, scrawny-looking and forlorn in the brittle heat and at midday they stopped to eat and rest, Talbot realizing that the wonderful coffee was only to be had from Louise.

While they ate, Max enlarged upon Saville's run of bad luck. Saville had been attacked about six weeks earlier, while riding the south sector with two of the hands. They had been ambushed near a spot known locally as White

Rock. The two hired men had been killed and Saville almost crippled. He had been pulled from his horse and dragged over a bed of shale, dislocating a hip and lacerating his legs so badly he almost bled to death. A homesteader, one of Saville's neighbours, had found him while out looking for his son who in turn had been out looking for the homestead's only milk cow, which had somehow gotten loose.

Then they'd had a stampede that almost levelled the house, the furious, thundering mass of crazed beef turning away from the front yard with less than a quarter mile to spare. Next, there was a fire in the cookhouse that killed the cook, the only man not in town at a dance. The best waterhole, that was to say the only one that never, ever dried, was polluted, had to be filled in and then some of the crew left one night, apparently bribed to do so. Now the crew was pared back to the barest minimum and there was a double workload for everyone.

The last two incidents had occurred on the very day of Talbot's arrival. Someone had released a full corral of freshly broken horses and two men had tried to kidnap Trisa.

'Let's just hope you've changed our luck, Nathan.'

'Let's just hope I haven't brought you more of the same.'

'You already changed our luck last night, with Trisa,' Max pointed out. Talbot nodded silently. It had not been compensation enough for Howard.

'You never said what it was made you change your mind and stay,' Max said innocently, starting to kill the remains of the fire, pouring the last of the coffee over the embers and then burying the rest under the sand.

'Mr Saville said I'd be replacing the son he'd lost.'

Max was surprised at the way Talbot said it, through his teeth and with a look in his eyes that spoke of things said between himself and Saville that would not bear repeating. He wondered what the mystery was. Talbot didn't offer to enlighten him.

'Anyway, that's the story so far. The Saville ranch has just about survived the worst of it.'

'I've just got one question,' Talbot said as he pushed himself to his feet.

'What's that?'

'I want to know what happened to the milk cow.'

10

Max's hopeful statement to Talbot that day that the Saville luck was about to change proved to be somewhat premature. At supper, as the family gathered for the evening meal in the dining-room, with its long refectory table and the best china and silver on display, Saville told them that the bank was about to foreclose.

Saville had borrowed the money seven months ago, before all the trouble started, to buy a small section of land lying northward, from a smallholder who wanted to try California. The land had two good waterholes and the house and outbuildings would be useful. Saville liked to employ married men when he could and the purchase would let him offer at least one family decent accommodation if they wanted it.

He had reckoned on paying the loan

back in full after his next cattle drive but the bank manager himself, Fletcher Curtis, had come out today to explain that they were to call it in. He would have to pay it all back in full within thirty days or the bank would take stock and property to recover its loss.

The news was a shattering blow to everyone. In a house where money had seldom been scarce, it was a frightening threat. Saville had absolutely no means of paying the loan back in thirty days.

Talbot was not there to hear the next bad luck instalment. When he arrived, shaved and bathed, in a fresh shirt and even with a bit of an appetite, the atmosphere of doom communicated itself to him at once. He sat down slowly, looking at the distressed faces and catching a look of bitter hatred from Saville, as if, somehow, it were his fault.

'Something wrong?' he asked.

'Nothing for you to concern yourself with,' Saville said harshly and Max looked at him in shocked surprise.

'We might have to sell the ranch, that's all, as if that's none of your concern, Nathan,' Max replied, though still looking at Saville.

'Dad borrowed money and the bank wants it back in thirty days,' Trisa explained, plainly worried by the prospect of being left homeless. The silence intensified until Talbot spoke, directly to Saville.

'Perhaps I can help. I have a little money.'

The head of the house looked up at him, unable to kill the flicker of hope in his eyes, before it was overshadowed by the more normal scorn he reserved solely for his new business partner.

'I need more than fifty bucks,' he snarled.

'How much have you got, Nathan?' Max asked, flicking a look of annoyance at Saville.

'How much do you need?'

Nobody knew the exact figure except Saville and for a few seconds he struggled, not wanting to tell him.

'Two thousand dollars,' he finally said. Talbot nodded calmly.

'Yes, I can raise that much all right,' he said and to his surprise Trisa gave a cheer, Louise and Max laughed with relief and Max leaned across the table to clap him on the back.

'I think everyone ought to calm down till we've seen Mr Talbot's money,' Saville said sternly but nobody paid any attention. It was as Max had said today. Talbot had come to change their luck.

In the morning Talbot rode with Max into Point Osborne. He identified himself at the very prosperous looking Mercantile Bank and with one of their cheque forms, filled in the amount owing, plus enough to pay the next month's wages, transferable from his own bank in Boston. They had to wait, while wires were sent and looks exchanged. It had been common knowledge that the Saville ranch was on the skids, that word had come down from the head office to foreclose on the Saville loan, an unheard of thing during fiscally prosperous times.

While they waited, Talbot took the time to send a brief wire to Sheriff Wells, letting him know he had arrived in one piece, after which they headed for the nearest bar, the Heart of Gold saloon, situated appropriately enough halfway along Gold Street. The saloon was just a place to get a drink. There was no attempt at entertainment for the paying customers, no piano, no feminine presence, nothing breakable on the bar or walls. The floorboards were sanded and the tables and chairs of the cheapest, plainest type.

'No expense spared,' Talbot murmured.

'Fella who owns this place doesn't believe in spending money where it's not needed. He owns the hotel too and a luncheon room.'

'What's the hotel like?'

'Like this, with carpets. Some men want frills and fancies, some just want to drown it all in beer. This bar takes care of the dedicated drinker.'

'Nobody could dedicate themselves to drinking this,' Talbot said after taking another cautious sip of the muddy looking beer. For days now, everything he drank seemed to taste bitter. Talbot saw that Max was looking thoughtful as he nursed his drink and he permitted himself a wry smile.

'I can see you're still wondering about me, Max.'

'I think I might be entitled to wonder how come you have nearly three thousand dollars just layin' around in a bank in Boston,' Max said with a slight shrug.

'It was just some money my grand-mother left me. She died during the first year of the war.'

'Uh-huh,' Max said and took a thoughtful pull on his beer.

They returned to the bank an hour later to find that his cheque had cleared. The bank manager was clearly embar-rassed. It had not been his decision to call in the loan. Talbot blandly accepted the flustered manager's apologies but as they were leaving, he casually asked Max, loud enough for anyone else to hear, if there was another bank in town. Max turned to look at Fletcher's white face and grinned. The Saville account had, until the last few months, been healthier than any other. If Saville took his business elsewhere, others might follow.

Max wanted to celebrate some more but Talbot wanted to leave. He had been watching all day for an angular, well-dressed gunman and his strapping curly-haired friend. He felt he was making too much of a target of himself. He had not forgotten their threat and he knew it would only be a matter of time before they made an attempt to carry it out.

He also knew that this business with the bank loan was connected somehow with those two and with the men who had hunted Trisa. Saville had a powerful enemy somewhere, someone with enough clout to squeeze a bank. Perhaps, he thought, as they rode home, the answer lay in all that paperwork Saville had threatened him with.

11

The waterhole was dry. Talbot knelt in the centre of the hollow which had, until recently, been full to the lip with water, and sifted a handful of the dampish earth. In a day or two it would resemble every other watering place within miles, cracked all across like a jigsaw and baked useless.

Talbot removed his hat to mop his forehead and the sun struck his bare head with staggering violence. He quickly replaced the hat, closing his eyes briefly till the dull throb of pain behind the retina was gone, and straightened from the day's second disappointment in time to catch a humourless smile from Max.

'We haven't had one this bad in some time,' he said. Talbot, with furrowed brow, looked around him at the scorched terrain with the air of a man trapped in a foreign country, where the language spoken was not his own, where the rules were harsh, barbaric compared to what he had known and as opposite in nature to his own set of values as day and night. He wondered if he would ever adjust to the brutal heat. But then hadn't his old friend Doctor Jerome always said that this was the ideal climate for him, warm and dry, with no damp to provoke his fever-prone blood?

He came up out of the dried-up bed of the waterhole and took the reins of the grey horse he now rode, a big, gentle mare, patient and calm in all situations, and began to walk for a little while to get the feel of the ground under his feet again.

And as he walked, betraying himself with an action no cattleman ever performed when he had a horse to ride, Max watched him with a dry smile. He liked Talbot. With one exception, there was no one in the least degree like him out here, certainly not on the ranch. He was an Easterner and educated and Max suspected that he had been army once, ranking army at that. The Saville foreman had ridden for the Union himself and he recognized first-class officer material when he saw it.

In the short time he had been on the ranch Talbot had earned the respect of most of the Saville crew, partially because he knew his way around horses as well as any of them. Horses had been his father's second passion, next to his business, and his stables were amongst the finest in Massachusetts. He had passed a good deal of his know-how and natural instinct on to his son. In this respect Talbot was already worth his weight in gold, someone who could rope and ride as well as the best of them, and better than most. But mainly they saw how hard he worked, driving himself at a wicked pace, savagely attentive to detail and on his feet through all the hours of daylight and beyond. He was a man driven, not allowing himself an idle moment to ponder his situation.

But it was not only his mania for work that impressed the crew. He was fair in his dealings with everybody, including Jack Spinner and Ray Murch, who were both inclined to bad mouth him behind his back. So long as they did their fair share of the work he didn't seem to mind their hostility.

He had made good on his threat to move the Saville bank account and after a brief, near monosyllabic discussion with Saville, took the account to the small Savings and Loan bank in Caldwell. Already that was paying dividends, with a better interest rate and one or two sweeteners from a bank anxious to keep an important new customer. He took care of the bills and paper work in half the time it had ever taken Saville, and he initiated one or two popular bonus schemes which the crew were mightily pleased with, since they were all working pretty damned hard. He found a married couple to occupy the premises on Saville's land purchase and gave the man a good chunk of the north side to take care of, a decision which proved to be a sound one. Andy Chase had been down on his luck, all the way down and worried sick about his young family. Suddenly he had a home, a good paying job and good prospects. It was little wonder that he set out with a will to prove to Talbot that he was worth the risk the Saville manager had taken.

Already the Saville fortunes were taking a turn for the better, though Talbot was too busy to notice that everyone put that improvement down to him.

He was not aware of the impression he made, only that he was accepted by them and that was all that mattered in the mean time. He knew that however friendly they might be to him now, if they were to find out about Howard, they would bury him. There were some still who remembered Howard with the kind of short-sighted affection that only time and distance and death can create.

They had liked the son of a bitch and now that he was dead, they had enshrined him.

Talbot and Saville played their little game and nobody was any the wiser. They were cool with one another but intensely polite. Never, since the day Talbot had wired his bank for money, had Saville shown again that bitter hostility that had so surprised Max and the others.

And he had found a true friend in Max Ryan. He liked the foreman, liked his dry sense of humour, his steadiness, his patient acceptance of a new manager who was, so far as cattle ranching was concerned, a complete tenderfoot, at least to begin with. Many another foreman as close to his employer as Max was to Saville would have resented Talbot's arrival. But there was no resentment, only friendship and a generously offered helping hand.

Then there was Trisa. From the first she had exhibited all the classic symptoms of an adolescent in love, and as time passed, Talbot managed to convince himself that it was simply a harmless infatuation that she would soon get over. He was unaware that his courteous, gentle dealings with her only made Trisa love him the more.

He was quite sure of his own feelings for her though and Trisa would have been shocked to know just how deep those feelings ran but he masked them thoroughly from everyone, determined that he would not be the cause of her being hurt.

He might have steered her affections away from himself more successfully if he had not been distracted by his new role as ranch manager, if he had not been loved and laundered and fed by Louise, who mothered everyone, if he had not been trying to adjust to being part of a family unit again, accepted and to a large extent needed by them. Otherwise he might have diverted the disaster that was to come, might have packed his leather grip that very day to move on.

But it was four weeks later and he was still here and knew that he would remain here until Saville had no further use for him. Four weeks closer to exposure and riding a parched parcel of land with Max, looking for water where there was none to find, for as Max had just said, there hadn't been a drought this deadly in four or five decades.

Max, with a tilt of the chin, indicated a couple of wheeling vultures in the distance.

'Most likely another dead steer,' he remarked as Talbot remounted and they began to ride towards the birds anyway, sure of what they would find, the emaciated carcass of a steer, dropped down for want of good grass and water. But they were wrong. Lying face down in a growing pool of her own blood, they found a woman.

Talbot reached her first. He turned her over and gently cradled her back and head, his eyes raking over her for the injury that had bled so badly. It wasn't hard to find, partly because her thin blue cotton dress had been pushed up over her waist, right up to her breasts, twisted tightly to one side and pushed almost under her armpit, leaving her all but naked. Despite the dress and the style of her hair, which had been wound into a knot at the nape of the neck, very much like the way Louise wore her hair, she was not a white woman. Her skin was dusky brown and her eyes almost the colour of jet, looking up at him with the shock and revulsion of the brutal assault she had endured still in them.

She had been stabbed, at least four times, low in the stomach and groin and from the bruises and fluids on her thighs, it looked like she had been raped too. Her face was bruised, and she had what looked like a burn mark on her neck, as if something had been tightened and then ripped away from her.

Talbot murmured soothing noises from a throat tight with anger and shock. He pulled a clean handkerchief from his shirt pocket and pressed it to the worst, the deepest of her wounds, then gently eased her dress down, for she was trying feebly to cover herself with her hands. She stared dully at Talbot's stricken face and said something which he recognized as Apache but did not understand. Max had brought his canteen, but now that he saw she had stomach wounds, he shook his head.

'She wants water.'

Talbot reached for the canteen. She was dying. A little liquid would not kill her any faster than those wounds. She drank gratefully, though most of it trickled back out of the side of her mouth.

'Ask her who did this?' Talbot said, without taking his eyes from her face. Max spoke to her quietly and she rolled her eyes to him, recognizing her mother's tongue, then she looked back at the one who held her so gently, whose face seemed to wish it could bear her pain. It was to Talbot she replied, perhaps thinking he could understand, speaking in a mixture of Apache and English that Max could barely follow.

She was drowning in her own blood. When she had finished speaking, she lay quiet, struggling inwardly against a desire to sleep and when she could fight it no longer, she turned her face against Talbot's shirt and passed away.

Talbot held her for a long time after she was dead, the brutality of what had been done to her rendering him inert, his mind suddenly filled with images of war and death, young men butchered like this but by guns and swords and cannon fire, their eyes like this girl's eyes, looking at him from under half-closed lids with sad reproof.

'Get my blanket will you, Max?' he asked.

'Leave her,' Max answered and his voice was different from the voice he had used to speak to the woman, harder somehow and cold. Talbot looked up in surprise to see Max looking nervously over his shoulder.

'What?'

'I said leave her. Let's go, now.'

'We can't.' Talbot was outraged. He knew he had left civilization behind but not that far behind.

'Do you know who she is?' Max demanded of him.

'How would I . . . no, I don't know who she is.'

'She's trouble, that's who. Gila's squaw.'

In the ensuing silence, Talbot finally got up to fetch the blanket himself. Max grabbed his arm.

'Leave her, for God's sake. Let Gila or one of his people find her. Don't let it be a white man that discovers this.'

'Why?'

'It's just . . . it would be a mistake. Take my word for it, Nathan, it would be a bad mistake.'

Gently but firmly disengaging his arm from Max's grip, Talbot unwound his blanket from the straps that secured it.

'I'm not leaving her here to be eaten by those birds.'

Max stubbornly refused to help roll the woman in the blanket, his arms folded, his mouth compressed angrily. Talbot worked alone, carefully wrapping the still pliant body and limbs in the brown blanket, tying it off twice with a length of twine.

'Who is this Gila anyway?' he asked Max when he was almost through.

'He's an Apache, a very, very bad *hombre*. There's only one thing he hates more than white men and that's rich white men like Saville. The boss thinks it was some of his men who attacked him that day. He might think this is some kind of revenge.'

'And leaving her lying out here is going to persuade him it wasn't?' Talbot asked with a pertinence that annoyed the hell out of Max.

'You're right,' he said grimly. 'We have to bury her somewhere.'

'Max,' Talbot said in a voice that brooked no denial, the unmistakable voice of a commanding officer. 'This woman, this *girl* has been murdered, on

Saville property. It has to be investigated. Or is that another old Eastern custom you've given up out here?'

Max was silent. He knew Gila's reputation. When crossed he was your worst nightmare come to life and all Max wanted right then was to be somewhere else. He knew Nathan was a reasonable man. All he had to do was find the key to what was bothering him here.

'Listen, Nate,' he said thoughtfully, and Talbot turned square to face him, waiting curiously to see what kind of tactics the foreman would use to make him change his mind. 'Why don't we bury her in a shallow grave right here? Then we can notify the authorities. She's got folks in Point Osborne. We can bring the sheriff out here tomorrow to fetch her back. We can't walk all the way to town and our horses have come too far today to carry two.'

On the face of it his suggestion seemed logical enough, but Talbot recognized it for the subtle shift in argument that it was and after a moment, wordlessly reached for the shovel on his saddle. Max, with a badly disguised sigh of relief helped spade the rock-hard ground into yielding a shallow space for the pathetic bundle in the blanket.

When it was done Talbot marked the grave with a small pyramid of stones, took off his hat to arm sweat from his face and then hunted around for something appropriate to say. Finally, all he could think of was the Lord's Prayer which he began to recite in his pleasant, slightly flat-vowelled Boston accent. Max offered a second, 'Amen' at the end and then they both turned away to stow their gear.

'What did she say, when she spoke to you, Max?'

'She said it was somebody she knew. I didn't catch it all. He was white, anyway, brought her here with some kind of trick then raped and stabbed her.'

'And left her lying out here in this

heat to bleed to death,' Talbot said, at a loss to understand such deliberate cruelty and evil. It was hard enough when you hurt people accidentally, he knew to his cost. What kind of conscience did the man have who had stabbed and killed a girl no older than Trisa?

12

Events conspired, however, to prevent Talbot from returning to the grave of the dead woman the next day. Word came in first thing next morning that there had been fences cut out at the north pasture. He and Max and three others rode out to see what was what and found themselves on a three-day cattle round-up.

Saville had some pretty decent neighbours though and some of them set to and helped round up the cattle that had strayed through the damaged fences, knowing that one day they might need that help themselves.

But it was clear that the fences had been deliberately sabotaged, the wires cleanly cut and Talbot wondered if it had been done as some kind of diversion. He was anxious to get back to the ranch to make sure all was well, a forlorn hope as it turned out.

At the ranch house they found more trouble. It was chow time but nobody was eating. Everyone was gathered at the stable block, looking in at something with grave, silent faces. Somebody came and took their horses away to cool them off and, with a glance at one another, they made their way towards the group. The men made a path for them and they went through the open door, into semi-darkness.

The familiar smells of hay and horses met Talbot as he paused to allow his eyes to adjust to the dimness. The shallow murmur of voices led him to a corner of the stable that was particularly shadowy. A storm lantern had been lit to guide the efforts of the man kneeling on the straw, who was obviously a doctor. As he had been making his way through the cluster of men, he had heard one of them say that it was Jud Willis, an old-time hand who worked permanently in the stables, that he had fallen out of the loft and had broken something.

Talbot looked at Jud and knew he had done more than that. There was a mess of blood everywhere. Yet another sudden, inexplicable death.

He made no sound. He stayed quietly back a little from the drama, watching the doctor's capable hands staunch and bind, while Trisa held the lantern for him, so that all the light fell in a strangely bleached circle on the dying man.

She looked up once at him with a great deal more calm than she felt, surprised by the look of concern on Talbot's face. A moment later it was over, something about the attitude of the doctor's back telling Talbot it was finished. Trisa looked up with a dumbfounded expression on her suddenly very young face.

'He's dead,' she said huskily. 'Jud . . . he's dead.'

'I'm sorry,' Talbot responded softly and the doctor, on his knees in the straw, stiffened at the sound of Talbot's voice and started to rise.

'How did it happ — ' Talbot bit off the last words as he came face to face with Doctor David Jerome.

At their last meeting, at the court martial, Talbot had been a very sick man, worn out with worry and guilt, his face fixed in an expression of frozen anguish. Confronted by this spectre from his own personal nightmare, Talbot's face looked just the same to the doctor.

Talbot felt as if he had been delivered a physical blow. Jerome was the last person he expected or wanted to see right then, and now the memories came rushing back on him, like an icy tide breaking on his back. But he managed a grim smile as he took the doctor's proffered hand.

'David,' he managed to get out of a constricted throat. 'You're working here then?'

'It's kind of a long story, Nathan,' Jerome said with a rueful smile, giving Talbot's hand a reassuring squeeze, then he turned away to begin organizing the removal of Jud, having two of the hands lift and carry out the body. Talbot watched them direct these operations for a while and then found himself drifting back, like a wreath of smoke caught in a breeze.

The rain had returned that day and the battle encampment was a brooding quagmire of mud and pooled water. People were coming and going with all the haste of an army in retreat, sorting itself out, casting around for the best bolt-hole. In any event there was little time for a trial of the kind that Talbot might have expected in time of peace. The matter was to be dealt with as swiftly and bloodlessly as possible.

Weakened badly by a relapse, he had to be helped to his place before the drum-head court and fortunately the last remnants of illness dulled and blunted the edges of the proceedings for him so that he was never very clear about what was said or by whom. Only one thing stood out and that was the way Doctor Jerome and Sergeant Lyons both spoke for him.

But their loyalty had no effect on the outcome. The final verdict left Talbot without a commission or a character. The phrase they used, 'Mustered out of service in disgrace', was one he would never forget. For him there was none of the humiliation of being stripped of rank. Somewhere along the way he passed out, from too long on his feet after too long on his back, his weakness aggravated by the persistent, cloying heat of the day. That aspect of it at least had been quite painless.

'Best not to go back on things,' Doctor Jerome advised, jolting him back from his recollections.

'I don't, not if I can help it.'

Jerome took his arm and steered him out of the stable, where there was a stench of blood, out into the fresh air. They both looked up at a changed sky, saw clouds banking there on the horizon and both knew that it was just a false alarm. Clouds had rolled up before, had taken one look at the parched land and had turned tail.

'Didn't you go home at all, Nathan?' Jerome was asking him.

'I didn't even consider it. Couldn't take something like that back to my mother.'

Jerome understood, since he knew Theodora Talbot. She was simply not the type to forgive an act that would diminish her social standing in any way. And that was exactly what the deaths of those men on Cherry Bridge would have meant to her. Her son might be haunted forever by his deed, his career might lie in ruins about his feet, but what did that matter against a snub at a luncheon party?

'And you, David? You had a home in Boston too.'

'Yes, I had a home there, but no family, most of my friends killed or scattered by the war. I knew I couldn't go back when it was all over, just knew I couldn't settle to city life again.' There had been someone back in Boston he would gladly have returned to but that was not something Talbot wanted to hear. 'I don't know if you're aware of this, Nathan, but I wrote to the families of those boys who were killed and explained . . . tried to explain what happened.'

'No, I didn't know,' Talbot said in a quiet voice.

'Naturally, I wrote to Saville and we struck up a friendship, kept on writing through the rest of the war. When I got my discharge, he asked me if I would consider coming out here to take up my practice. Haven't regretted my decision for a minute.'

'I wonder if they know how lucky they are,' Nathan said and Jerome smiled at the compliment. He had never bothered to tell Saville that he was one of the finest surgeons in Boston before the war. His eyes thoughtful, he measured his next words very carefully.

'I was the one who brought you here, I suppose you know that,' he said and he took a half-step back to watch the effect of his words. Talbot plainly did not understand and for a while the only expression on his face was mild curiosity, his head inclined slightly as he tried to register what the doctor had said.

'What do you mean?'

'I told those lawyers where to find you, Lyle's lawyers. When Saville told me they were looking for you, I told them where you were.'

'In God's name why?'

'Why do you suppose?'

'You brought me here, to the house of the man I killed? What kind of a barbarian are you?'

Talbot kept his voice low, but his anger was fierce, barely controlled.

'Now don't call me any more names till you know the facts, Nathan. Come into my office tonight and we'll talk.'

Talbot could scarcely speak for indignation. The doctor's brown eyes regarded him calmly.

'It had better be good, Doctor.'

'Well, go on in the house and have your supper now. I'll see you later, won't I?'

'Oh, you can count on it,' Talbot said heatedly. And with a last blistering, uncharitable stare at the doctor, he wheeled away and strode back towards the barn.

Trisa watched him walking towards her, surprised by the fact that Talbot and the doctor seemed to know one another and by the angry look on Talbot's face, his eyes gone the flat, cold colour of a sky with thunder in it. She was so used to his habitual expression of tired amiability that this new look startled her.

His expression softened as soon as he saw her, his hand coming to rest on her shoulder.

'Are you all right?' he asked and she nodded, warmed by his concern, pleased that he wanted to spare her the violence of Jud's death.

'I found this in the straw, just by Jud's hand,' she said, holding out the

125

object, a broken silver chain with a small, neatly fashioned charm resembling a bird in flight.

'Did you ever see him wearing this?' he asked. Trisa shook her head and Talbot put the necklace in his pocket. 'I'll check his personal things in the safe to see if he has any family.'

'You can check,' she said, falling into step beside him as he walked back to the house, 'but he never had any family. I asked him once but he said no, they'd all died a long time ago.'

She looked at Talbot's face and wanted to ask this deeply personal man about his family, about his life before he came here but he looked so remote and distant that she hesitated and the moment was lost.

13

The grey horse threw a shoe as it carried him into Caldwell after supper, forcing him to make a short detour to the livery stable to arrange for repairs before setting out to find the doctor.

Jerome's office was a fairly substantial building by Caldwell standards, the lower half split in two between the doctor's surgery and waiting-room in one half and the stagecoach offices in the other. All of the upstairs part of the building belonged to Jerome, three bedrooms, a decent sized parlour that looked out on to a carefully tended back garden, and a dining room and kitchen. The attic space had been converted to living quarters for the married couple who looked after the doctor. Mrs Florence Addie, who was his housekeeper and cook and her husband Bill, who did odd jobs, tended the garden and looked after his stable.

Jerome had been watching for him and was waiting in the parlour with a drink in either hand. Talbot put his hat down on a side table and sank down listlessly on to the davenport sofa that sat underneath the open window, feeling the ponderous weight of the heat more than usual tonight. He accepted the drink with thanks.

'You look tired, Nathan,' Jerome remarked. 'Not coming down with a little bout are you?'

Talbot had been looking around at the old-fashioned furnishings, some of them obviously brought all the way from Boston, heavy, polished expensive pieces that fitted comfortably into Jerome's large upstairs parlour. He felt at home here amongst these things that were as much a part of his own past as Jerome's. Indeed he recognized one or two items from the days when he had visited Jerome's home. Both of David's parents had died from an outbreak of typhus when he was still a very young man. Talbot had often wondered if that had been the incentive for him to enter the medical profession.

At the doctor's question, he looked around and answered shortly, as he always did when questioned upon the tricky subject of his health.

'I haven't been sick since the winter,' he said, wondering bleakly if he would see another winter of bludgeoning fever, as helpless and alone as he had been last November.

'I suppose you think I'm a bastard,' Jerome suggested.

'You don't want to know what I think,' Talbot said without any attempt at humour and he swallowed the doctor's good whiskey down. Jerome stepped forward and filled his glass again.

'I acted for the best. You legally own half of that spread, you know. You are entitled to it.'

Talbot's silence was not encouraging. Jerome drank his own drink and took a seat opposite him. He had been rehearsing his little speech all night but now the words had no meaning in the face of Talbot's battened down anger and sense of betrayal.

'They don't know who you are,' he tried gently.

'Saville knows.'

'Sure he knows, but he needs you and as long as he needs you he won't tell anyone else.'

'We both know,' Talbot said, leaning forward with his forearms on his thighs, 'what a son of a bitch Howard Saville was under my command. But out here he was everybody's blue-eyed boy. If they ever find out just how that conniving lieutenant of mine died, there won't be enough of me left to crate.' He paused to swallow his second drink more deliberately. 'Besides, I wouldn't hurt those people, not for anything. Saville can have my share of the ranch and I'll be on my way.'

'It's only for another month, Nathan. Greg will be back on his feet and running things in four, maybe six weeks, I promise you. Four weeks for you to find out who's trying to run Saville off.'

'They're just having a run of bad luck,' Talbot said, but involuntarily he thought of the two men on the train and Trisa and the strange behaviour of the bank manager, Curtis Fletcher.

'You don't believe that any more than I do,' Jerome said, realizing that he had hooked Talbot. Slowly, gently, he began to reel him in. 'Of course, I've no real proof and I haven't told anybody else this, but Jud's the second man I've been called out to that I thought had been murdered.'

Talbot stood up. He was sweating and he could feel the heat and alcohol beginning to muddle him. He paced to the fireplace and rested his right foot on the fender. Jerome joined him there, leaning a shirt-sleeved elbow on the mantelshelf.

'My theory, for what it's worth, is that Jud was attacked in the hayloft and then somebody finished him off on the ground, with an axe I think. He had damaged ribs and a broken wrist, as if he tried to save himself when he fell and Trisa says he was face down when she arrived, but the blow that killed him was to the back of the skull. He landed on soft straw, with no hard or blunt object near him, yet his head was split wide open. I think he was trying to get to his knees when his killer finished him off.'

The two of them stood in silence for a moment, both thinking of the bloody mess Jud had made. Jerome silently topped up Talbot's glass and absently he swallowed it down.

'Time to find out what's going on, Nathan. There's somebody on the ranch with a powerful grudge, who has killed twice and tried to kidnap and maybe kill Trisa. You're on the inside. You've the right to ask some questions, take a look at Saville's papers. Maybe somebody stands to make out of Saville's death and Trisa's disappearance. That, my friend, is why I brought you here. You're the only one I can trust.'

Talbot stared rather blearily at the doctor. He realized he was a little drunk. He had not eaten much supper and the whiskey had gone to work on a virtually empty stomach. Louise was constantly trying to cure his lack of appetite with good food and a mother's care but seeing David Jerome today had killed all desire to eat.

'David, how did you know where to find me?'

'I've known where you were since the trial, more or less. Owed it to your father I suppose, to keep my eye on you. I meant it for the best when I told those lawyers where you were Nathan.'

'Knowing that once I got here, I wouldn't have any choice except to stay, what with my guilty conscience and all.'

'I counted on you having a conscience, yes.'

Talbot took the whiskey out of Jerome's hand and poured himself a generous measure. As he tilted the glass, his eye fell on the tin-type standing on the shelf at Jerome's elbow, similar to the one on Saville's desk. Indeed it had been taken on the same day and by the same photographer.

It showed a young captain, sober as cold water, hat under arm, handsome and remote, unaware of destiny's trap-door, yawning in front of those smartly polished riding boots.

'Easy to forget how damned young we all were then. I didn't think you'd mind me keeping this,' Jerome smiled.

'No, of course not.'

'I know how your mother felt, but what about Dolly and Irene?'

'I don't know. Why should my sisters react any differently from Mother?' he said tersely, and Jerome saw how tender he was on this subject still. He started to speak, changed his mind, took the whiskey back and drained the last of it into the two glasses.

'Maybe you'd be surprised,' he said, raising the glass to his lips but taking only a brief sip. There was something he needed to tell Talbot but maybe he had had enough shocks for one evening.

Talbot looked at the photograph on the doctor's mantelshelf. When that had been taken he had been a young man with a future, quite a promising one too. He had a family, a mother who was possessively proud of him despite his lowly rank and two lovely, adoring young sisters, numerous aunts and uncles and cousins, plenty of friends. Not only had the deaths at Cherry Bridge affected *his* future, it had affected theirs. He had decided not to go home to spare them as much as himself. He swallowed the last of the whiskey and set the glass down.

'Nothing in this world will ever surprise me again, David,' he said and, reaching for his hat, he turned and left.

14

Outside it was already completely dark, the sky full of thin rainless clouds. Talbot walked directly to the livery stables to collect his horse, calling at the open door for George, the stable hand who had promised to shoe the grey. There was no reply. He began passing down along the stalls with the same unthinking ease that had trapped Trisa. When he tripped and went sprawling on the floor, he thought he had fallen foul of a broom or rake handle, but when he started to rise, hands were laid on him. He felt himself hustled to his feet and was dragged towards the open-sided part of the building where the blacksmith worked.

A shade breathlessly, he took stock of the four faces ranged around him, one on each corner of his person, two on either side of the glowing, red-hot forge. Castle, Billy, Baker and Conrad. For an insane thirty seconds he tried to fight his way out of it, but he fought like a man with four or five hefty tumblers of whiskey inside him, too slowly and not enough.

His struggle surprised and at first alarmed them for he all but managed to tear loose, but there were four of them, and Castle was armed. The .45 stilled Talbot. In the face of that cold, dark maw he allowed them to jostle and rearrange him more to their liking. The gun was lowered but not replaced in Castle's holster. It dangled from the gunman's fist in a practiced, professional fashion.

'Now, you didn't do like we told you,' Castle said, pressing the barrel of the gun hard into Talbot's side. 'We told you to leave. Don't you remember us telling you that?'

'I thought you were ticket collectors,' Talbot said, sounding bored. 'You said I'd get a refund.'

Castle hit him a back-handed punch that drew blood. Talbot staggered, was righted by the men holding him and braced himself for the follow-up blow.

'That punched your ticket,' Baker laughed. Billy picked up the blacksmith's poker and jammed it into the hot coals of the forge.

'You're a lucky man,' Castle said to him as he twisted the poker in the embers. 'You-all get a second chance. Next time we won't warn you.'

'Next time, next time, don't you clowns ever get anything right the first time,' Talbot goaded with acid scorn but Castle refused to rise to the bait. He holstered his gun and pulled the iron out of the fire, holding it in a gloved left hand. The tip was a smoky, dull red, crusted with hot ash.

'Give me his arm,' he said softly, pleasurably. Billy and Conrad both hauled Talbot's left arm out, shoving back the cuff of the blue work shirt he wore.

'Here comes your refund.'

'Why you cheap, little hustler, running errands is all you're good for. You couldn't walk down the street without your hired muscle at your back.'

'You talk too much,' Baker hissed in his ear. 'I told you to mind your nose.'

'The iron's gettin' cold,' Billy pointed out and Castle gave a nod but got no further.

All hell broke loose around them. There were shouts, shots were fired, a stampede of booted feet, more shots. It sounded as if the whole town had arrived to help, just like that night with Trisa. Billy, with a dumb look from side to side, turned and blundered out into the night, followed by the two who had been holding Talbot.

Only Castle held his ground, his eyes sick with frustrated rage. He had been given strict instructions that Talbot was to be persuaded, not badly hurt, but something about him made Castle hate him. His defiance, his fearlessness and stupid jokes when he had a gun in his face were like salt ground into a wound. That was the thing that stuck in his craw. Talbot wasn't afraid of him.

He lunged at Talbot with the poker, aiming for the face. Talbot threw up his bared right arm to protect himself and the iron seared the flat of his wrist, singeing the flesh with an angry hiss. Castle dropped the poker and followed the others running.

Talbot staggered, clutching at his wrist, gone very white with the pain. Max reached him and Talbot looked mutely back at the foreman, realizing that he was alone, had managed to make his rescue sound like the arrival of a dozen.

'Thanks,' he murmured. Max gently prised Talbot's fingers away from the burn and looked at it closely.

'Jesus,' he grimaced, lifting his eyes to Talbot's still chalky face. 'Won't you ever stop walking into dark barns on your own?'

'I didn't know you were coming into town, Max,' he said, turning his shirt cuff back carefully from the rapidly blistering wound.

'No?' Max said, lifting his eyebrows.

'Well, I'll bet you're glad I did. Are you all right? You look a little stunned.'

'Yes,' Talbot said in a flat, tired voice. 'Would you get my hat for me, Max? I think it fell over there.'

'Sure, I see it. You can't lose Trisa's hat, for God's sake. What did they want anyway?'

'They wanted to frighten me.'

'Did they?' Max grinned.

'Yes,' Talbot grinned back.

'Was that the two from the train you told me about?'

'And the two who attacked Trisa.'

Max was silent as he absorbed the implications of this. Just then, George the stableman arrived with two other men, ready for trouble.

'What's all the commotion? We heard shots.'

'Rats, George. There were some rats in your feed bin,' Max said. 'Where the hell have you been anyway?'

'I'd just finished with Mr Talbot's horse when I got a note to say I was needed at home. But the wife didn't

141

know nothin' about it.'

'Come on, Nathan, let's go see Doc Jerome,' Max said, giving George the same look he had given Trisa that night when she'd produced her note.

Jerome was surprised and a little bit alarmed to see both of them.

'We ran into a little trouble at Casey's livery. Can you take a look at Nathan's arm while I go bring our horses around?'

As soon as Max was gone, Talbot held out the wrist for him. Jerome bent over it, shaking his head while Talbot briefly explained.

'Maybe I was wrong, Nathan,' Jerome said thoughtfully.

'About what?'

'About asking you to stay on here. You seem to draw trouble the way a magnet draws iron filings.'

Talbot laughed ruefully but Jerome's face was serious and concerned.

'I mean it, Nathan. You're going to have to be careful, more careful than tonight. What did they try to do, brand you? This is a bad burn.'

Talbot clenched his teeth as Jerome ministered to the burn with lotion and bandage.

'I'm afraid I had a little too much whiskey to see it coming,' he said, nodding to the almost empty bottle on the mantelshelf. 'But I don't intend to let them get me a third time.'

'Third time?'

'They were on the train when I came here. They warned me to leave and then threw me over the side. Damn near broke my neck.'

Jerome concentrated on binding the wrist, head down. It had all seemed so simple and clear cut over a civilized glass or two of whiskey. Max came back into the room.

'How is he?'

'He'll have a scar I shouldn't wonder,' Jerome said cryptically. 'All done now, Nathan. I'll see you in a day or two to change the dressing. Take care of yourself.'

'Do my best,' Talbot smiled at his friend.

At the window, Jerome watched the two men mount up and ride away, returning Max's salute with a raised hand. Talbot's head was bowed, his eyes closed. That burn would be hurting like hell, Jerome knew.

'What the hell have I done?' he asked himself.

15

Louise and Trisa waited on the veranda that night for the return of the two men, Louise sewing by the lamp, Trisa balanced on the veranda rail, swinging her legs and watching the dark approaches. She heard them ride in before she saw them, for Talbot had instigated a patrol between dusk and dawn and anyone approaching the house was required to give a signal. As Talbot dismounted, she saw at once the clean white stuff of the bandage on his wrist.

'What happened?' she cried in alarm, jumping down to go meet them. Talbot handed his reins to Max and turned to her, with the same troubled look in his eyes that had been there earlier in the day.

'My horse threw a shoe,' he said with a half-hearted smile, 'and me.'

'Are you in any pain?'

'Yes,' he answered truthfully, for she could see for herself that he was. Louise came down the steps, ready to fuss.

'It's just a graze,' he said quickly, forestalling her sympathetic movement towards him.

'You haven't broken anything, have you?'

'Just my pride,' he smiled, 'when I landed.'

'Come inside and I'll make some coffee.'

'Thanks, Louise, but I think I'll just turn in.'

'All right,' she said reluctantly. 'I'll send Max up with a cup for you, with a little brandy in it. It'll help you sleep.' She turned for the house, thinking that she would winkle the truth out of Max, because those two had been up to something tonight, nothing surer, and wild horses wouldn't drag it out of Nathan.

He followed Louise into the house, parting from her at the stairs, which, a shade wearily, he started to climb. He glanced back in annoyance when he saw Trisa following him. Entering his room, he dropped down gratefully on to the bed. Trisa stood by the open door, one hip on the door jamb, arms folded.

'Where did all this happen then?' she asked him.

'Just outside of Caldwell.' He lay with eyes closed, willing her to go away.

'Was Max with you?'

'No. We met up at the livery stable.'

After a long pause, she took a decisive step into the room.

'You're lying,' she told him flatly. 'I don't believe you fell off your horse. You never fell off a horse in your whole life.'

He opened his eyes and rolled his head around to look at her, too sickened by what had happened to feel like a rally with her. He knew from experience that once Trisa got her teeth into something, she would worry it for hours, days.

'Go to bed, Trisa.'

'Let me see that 'graze',' she

demanded, for she was convinced that it been caused by a gunshot or knife wound. Abruptly he got up from the bed and with two swift strokes, ripped away Doctor Jerome's gauze. She looked down at the ointment smeared burn, which was the breadth of the wrist and forked, like a snake's tongue, for the poker had made contact twice.

'All right?' he asked her severely.

'You said you fell,' she insisted.

'Go to bed, Trisa,' he implored her as he awkwardly tried to retie the bandage.

'Nathan,' she said in a tone of severely tried patience, 'I'm going to be twenty soon. You don't have to keep on protecting me like a helpless baby. If it was those two in the barn you can tell me. I won't faint.'

He continued to tie the bandage in silence. She batted his good hand away and took over, unwinding, then more carefully and gently rewinding the twisted bandage, till it was neat and flat and better than when Jerome tied it.

'If you don't tell me, Max will,' she said, not letting go of his hand and wrist, her eyes searching his face for clues.

'All right, Trisa. I walked right into it. Max was behind me and stopped them doing anything worse than this.'

'Bastards,' she swore under her breath, ignoring Talbot's upraised eyebrows. She turned his arm slightly, palm up and then with almost painful tenderness, rested her cheek against the bandaged flat of his wrist.

'I'm so sorry,' she whispered. 'If anything happened to you . . . '

Talbot did not speak or move, every muscle in his body tensing as her silky hair brushed against the skin above the bandage. Then she drew a long breath and straightened up.

'I told Max to follow you,' she admitted. 'I told him you'd gone to see the doctor and . . . well . . . we both wondered why.'

He stared at her in disbelieving silence and she stared him out.

'That wasn't a very ladylike thing to do, Trisa.'

Unable to meet his cold, hostile gaze, she dropped her eyes for a moment, and then raised them again defiantly.

'We just wanted to know how come you knew Doc Jerome, that's all. And why you were so angry after — '

'When we've finished with the inquisition,' he cut in savagely and she drew back from him, stung by the dry, hard note in his voice.

'Don't be angry with me,' she said but he did not relent.

'Go ahead,' he said coldly. 'Ask what you want. I've got no special privileges around here. As far as you're concerned, I'm just another hand on the payroll.'

He hated her concern and her questions and just at that moment he hated her for being who she was.

'I didn't mean to . . . don't be angry.'

'I'm not angry. Go to bed,' he repeated tonelessly. He sat down on the bed to take off his boots and when he looked up again she was gone.

He stripped and gave himself a cursory wash and crawled into bed, feeling more beat up by those five minutes with Trisa than by the whole attack in the barn. When Max came up with the coffee Louise had made, he feigned sleep, to avoid further conversation and maybe more questions. Max turned down the lamp and when he was gone, Talbot rolled on to his side, pressing the throbbing wrist against himself, comforted oddly by the heat and pain in it, trying not to dwell on a young girl's cheek resting on it and her hair brushing the hairs of his arm.

His last thought before sleep claimed him was that he had still done nothing about the murdered girl, lying in her shallow grave. He was asleep before he had drawn a dozen shallow breaths, the last gruelling forty-eight hours finally catching him up. He slept like a dead man till ten o'clock the next day.

16

The day of Trisa's birthday party dawned with a promise of heat, cruelly realized as the morning progressed. Talbot was up and dressed and gone before anyone, without even taking that reviving first cup of Louise's coffee. It was the end of the month and he had much business to take care of in Point Osborne for Saville.

At around eleven, he made his way to the sheriff's office to report something he had been neglecting, the murder of the young girl he and Max had found. The sheriff lounged in a swivel chair behind his desk, not bothering to get up when Talbot walked in, and right away, Talbot decided he didn't care for the man.

He was tall, big-boned, looked like he could take care of himself in a scrap, but his eyes were pouchy and bloodshot and, worryingly, considering the time of day, the smell of stale liquor hung on him. His clothes however were clean and neatly pressed, expensive-looking, and his leather vest and holster were of very fine, soft leather. A gold signet ring glinted on his pinkie and another on his right ring finger.

Talbot explained why he had come and Sheriff Arliss stared at him as if he had started speaking Chinese.

'You want me to investigate the death of a half-breed squaw?' he asked incredulously. When Talbot sat very still, not responding, his eyes wintry with anger, the sheriff gave a shrug and pulled a notepad out of a drawer to write down the details. That done, he tossed the pad back into the drawer with enough insolence to make Talbot want to mash his boot into the big man's face.

'Well, I'll be sure to get right on that, sir,' he drawled, returning to reading the local news sheet. Talbot stood up to leave, got as far as the door but then turned and returned to the desk.

'You do that, Arliss,' he said, leaning forward with his hands on the edge of the desk. 'And when the next child gets raped and murdered, I hope she isn't some innocent little white girl from the right side of the tracks. I'd hate to think what the citizens of this town might do when they find out you didn't think the matter warranted your attention.'

Arliss sat upright in his chair, his whole demeanour changing like lightning. He didn't like being criticized but he had a healthy regard for his own skin and he had already been told that Talbot was no pushover.

'I don't need you to tell me how to do my job,' he snarled as Talbot stalked out of the office, slamming the door behind him hard enough to rattle the windows. Arliss stared after him for a minute then the muscles in his face slackened and he leaned back in his chair. He opened the drawer with the notepad, read what he had written, a single scrawled sentence with the words

Fucking retard, then tore the sheet into four, balled it in one hand and tossed it at the wastebasket and missed before reaching deeper into the drawer for the whiskey bottle at the back.

Talbot was so angry, he had crossed town and reached his destination before he knew where he was. He had come to the other side of the railroad tracks, to the shanty town that had sprung up when the railroad was being built and had never quite gone away. Talbot roamed its narrow, dirty streets in search of someone who knew the dead girl, mentioning the name Max had given him, Gila. He met only silence and blank looks. Sometimes he saw fear in the eyes of the various Chinese, Mexican and Indians he asked and once or twice astonishment, as if he were mad to even ask. Nobody knew Gila, nobody knew his woman. Eventually he gave up, turning back to the town to fetch his horse. He gave the shanty town a last backward look and thought to himself that it was a pity

Point Osborne was turning into this kind of town, with the well-to-do side of it deliberately turning its back on the poorer district.

He had one other chore to deal with and at around one o'clock he arrived in Caldwell, which he found infinitely preferable to Point Osborne, a quieter, cleaner town altogether. He was sodden with sweat and had a dull, familiar pain between the shoulder blades. Unable to endure the brutal heat any longer, he went for cover, crossing the hostile area of naked road and climbing the stairs to Jerome's office.

In the doctor's front parlour the blinds were half-drawn, an old half-case clock ticked away the heavy, heat-laden minutes and Doctor Jerome came to greet him with a cold beer. He had just finished his midday meal but from the look of Talbot, knew there was no point in offering him some of the chicken left in the pot. Looking him over quickly, without appearing to do so, his professional eye noted with concern his colour and listlessness as he sank down on to the davenport under the window, the coolest place in the room.

'How's the wrist?' he asked, sitting down in his favourite battered and patched old leather wing-back chair that faced the sofa. Talbot leaned back, catching a little of the hot draught off the street.

'Itchy,' he replied and Jerome nodded.

'I'll change that dressing for you.'

'Thanks, David. No hurry.'

'You've been pretty busy, I hear. Trisa told me you were gone before breakfast this morning.'

'When did you see Trisa?'

'I just got back from the ranch an hour ago. Went out to give Greg the once over. Even he said he thought you were working too hard.'

'I do what's necessary, Doctor. The harder I work, the quicker I can leave.'

'It isn't necessary to kill yourself, Nathan.'

Talbot drained his glass, frowning slightly at the bitter taste of the beer.

'How is Mr Saville anyway?'

'He's making good progress. It's Trisa I'm worried about. She seems to think you're angry with her about something.'

Talbot's response was a terse silence.

'She said she sent Max after you that night, because she was curious as to our relationship,' Jerome said.

'Uh-huh, you see? Now it starts.'

'She said you were mad as hell, accused her of conducting an 'inky' something or other.'

'God, I didn't say that, did I?' Talbot asked, laughing in spite of himself.

'She has total recall where you're concerned,' Jerome said with a dry smile and Talbot sighed and made a gesture of helplessness with one hand.

'You know I haven't encouraged . . . '

'I know. I told her to forget it; you'd a temper like blazes but only let loose every August.'

Talbot was not sorry he had lost his temper with Trisa for the argument had done its work, created a small but sturdy barrier between them for which he was grateful. The very idea that she might come to care for him too much and then find out the truth about him was not to be contemplated. Better to keep her at arm's length altogether and avoid all future pain.

Jerome finished his own drink and came forward with fresh salve and bandages. He removed the slightly grubby cloth and looked closely at the still raw, red wound.

'That's coming along just fine,' he nodded and then proceeded to dress it again. 'Are you feeling all right? Otherwise, I mean?'

'I get tired easily lately. The heat I guess. That's all,' he admitted with a smile. David Jerome was immune to the charm in the smile. He knew it was turned on as often as not to divert unwanted questions and it generally worked on the likes of Trisa and Louise.

'I want you to ease off a little, Nathan,' Jerome said seriously. 'Eat something once in a while and get in a few early nights.'

'I get enough of that from Louise. If I ate everything she put on my plate I'd be the size of a house. And who sleeps in this heat?' He stood up, flexing his fingers under the new bandage. 'I'd better get back. Will I see you tonight at the birthday party?'

'I'll try but I've got an expectant mother coming near her time and another patient coming near the end of his. Barring labour and sudden death I should get there eventually.'

Talbot laughed softly, shook the doctor's hand and took his leave.

It was no cooler outside. He stuck to the shade, heading for the gunsmith's shop, to pick up Trisa's birthday gift. While he was there, waiting while the proprietor served another customer, he happened to glance out of the window.

The hairs on the nape of his neck prickled unpleasantly when he saw Baker cross the street, about to enter the saloon. He paused under the shade afforded by the saloon porch and Talbot saw that he was speaking to someone who stood there. Talbot moved away from the counter, moving slightly to one side of the window, watching the big man with the ugly, prize-fighter's face, reminded suddenly of that night in the barn when Trisa was so nearly lost to them, crushed and raped and God knows what else by those two men, but especially this man. He was busy telling the other something, his hands working, making slicing movements in the air. The other man nodded, and then laughed, his laughter carrying across the breadth of the street to Talbot. They both went into the saloon a moment later but not before the other man turned, giving Talbot a clear view of his face. Talbot paid for his purchase and left, wondering what Max would make of what he had seen.

On the way home he took a little detour to the spot where they had buried the girl. The little cairn Talbot had made had been kicked away, the stones scattered. The grave was empty.

It looked to Talbot as if the soil had been disturbed just recently and the slight, blanket wrapped occupant removed. Talbot stared down into the shallow depression he and Max had carved out of the unyielding ground and uneasily wondered who had known where to find her and who had dug her up.

17

It was just getting dark when Talbot rode into the yard. Lanterns had been strung and lit and a faint current of warm air made them lift and sway. Tables stood laden with food and there were barrels of beer to drink and bowls of fruit punch. Louise and her two helpers must have worked flat out to get everything ready, Talbot thought, as he stopped to admire the effect on the normally busy, businesslike yard.

One of the hands took his horse for him and he went directly upstairs to change. A hip bath had been thoughtfully filled for him and the water was still warm. He shaved and had a brief soak, before changing into his best clothes, which consisted of a pair of black pants from a once very good quality suit, a linen shirt with full sleeves, plain fronted, cool and clean-feeling and the vest of another black suit that nevertheless matched the pants well enough. He was pulling on his best boots when Max knocked and came into the room. He was shaven and dressed in his best too.

'You got here at last,' he said, leaning a hip against the bureau while Talbot tugged on his boots. 'A certain young person has been a little anxious that you wouldn't get back in time.'

Talbot stood and began looking through the bureau drawers.

'I saw one of the men who attacked Trisa today,' he said casually, moving aside Louise's neatly ironed shirts in search of his good neckcloth, a broad strip of black velvet that he eventually found and began to wind and tie, chin tilted, eyes on the mirror. Behind him, Max waited patiently for the rest of it.

'He was talking to someone, just outside the saloon.'

'In Caldwell?' Max asked.

'I was there to see the doctor. He wanted to have a look at my wrist. The someone he was talking to came to take

164

my horse for me in the yard just now.'

'You saw Trisa's attacker talking to somebody who works here, on this ranch?' Max asked flatly.

'Uh-huh. Haven't tied this thing since — '

'Who is he?'

Talbot's eyes shifted from his own reflection in the mirror to Max, who looked like somebody had lit a fire under him. He wondered if he should have kept this information to himself, dealt with it himself. But it was too late now.

'Doctor Jerome thinks that Jud and that other man, Mitchum, were murdered.'

'I've had my suspicions,' Max nodded.

'So last night I went through the books, checked the hirings and firings, and the man who took my horse tonight is one of three men who've been here as long as you've had trouble. He arrived just before the first accident.'

'Who is he?' Max asked again, trying

to keep a lid on his fury.

'Max, we haven't got a shred of proof,' Talbot said, abandoning his tie and moving to prevent Max from leaving the room, closing the door and standing with his back to it.

'This isn't Boston, Nate. We look after the law ourselves out here.'

'Not while I'm around you don't,' Talbot told him forcefully. 'I know how you take care of the law out here and I don't like it much.'

'And what if he is a killer?' Max argued heatedly.

'What if he's not?'

'We could go on like this all night. I say we do something about it now.' Talbot saw that Max's fists were bunched, his body inclining forward urgently.

'All right. We kick him off the ranch tonight and tell him that if he shows his face around here again he's all yours. He can't do any more harm around here and right now that's all I'm concerned about.'

'Not good enough,' Max gritted.

'What's the alternative?'

'We take him to the sheriff — '

'Arliss?' Talbot gave a grunt of scorn. 'And with what evidence? Just because I saw him talking to somebody? Or because he's been on the ranch for exactly six months?'

Max conceded, after a brief struggle with himself, slackening his bunched fists and with a little sigh, began to fix Talbot's tie for him, his big knuckles jabbing at the underside of Talbot's chin.

'We do it your way, for now. But I don't have to like it. Now are you ever gonna tell me who it is?'

'Ray Murch.'

'Oh yeah, Mr Murch. He was the one who came up to the house for help when Jud fell, according to Trisa. Come on, I just saw him go in the bunkhouse.'

The bunkhouse was an 'L' shaped building, with a dormitory filled with beds in one area and a dining and seating area in the other. Murch was still there when Max and Talbot entered. He was alone in the long narrow sleeping area, standing by his bunk. Talbot stood by the door while Max walked up to the man and confronted him. The bed separated them, a low iron cot, with a rolled up mattress, a folded blanket and bed linen on top of it. Murch's parcel of sparse belongings stood beside these, evidence that he had been about to leave.

He looked up without fear at the two men and smiled at them, his pale blue eyes unwavering. Murch was short, stocky, with a powerful neck and shoulders, big hands and a sharp, intelligent face that saw humour in every situation.

'Somethin' I can do for you, Mr Ryan?' he asked in his reedy, high-pitched voice, his eyes sweeping back to where Talbot stood.

'You leaving, Murch?'

'That's right.'

'Mighty sudden decision.'

'Man's entitled,' he shrugged, but

continued to stare at Talbot, whose uneasiness suddenly intensified. He moved away from the door and walked down along the line of beds till he was almost behind Murch, who followed his progress, then laughed once, a short, unpleasant barking sound and Talbot suddenly knew that the thing he had dreaded was going to happen here and now. Murch knew all about Cherry Bridge and he was about to tell Max.

'You're due some pay, Murch. Come on up to the house for it before you leave,' he said and he saw scorn in Murch's face. He wanted to break his fist against the hired man's face.

'Wait a minute now, Nathan. Murch and me got something to settle.'

'Leave it, Max,' Talbot said sharply and he started for the door.

'Hold on, Nate. I want to — '

'I said leave it.' He and Max glared at one another, Max baffled and angry but finally, reluctantly submissive. It was a sign of how much he had come to trust Talbot that he backed down when he did and turned from the room in his wake. Outside he took a hold on Talbot's arm, stopping him and jerking him around to continue the argument at close quarters.

'What the hell happened in there? You backed down from him. Why?'

'Nothing happened. We came down to fire him and he saved us the trouble.'

'No, that's not all that happened, Nate.'

'You'll find out soon enough,' Talbot said, kneading the back of his neck with his hand, clearly unhappy about something.

'Find out what, for God's sake? What are you being so damned secretive about?'

'You said we'd do it my way, Max,' Talbot reminded the foreman and without waiting for his reply, walked back to the house.

In the library, he opened the safe and counted out the necessary bills to make up Murch's pay. Behind him, he heard the door open and close and turned, his eyes tightening with shock.

The dress was pale yellow, full skirted, in a style that had been fashionable in Boston fifteen years since. It hugged her waist and accented her breasts. Her mother had bought it in fact ten years before on a rare trip back East. The straight, short hair had been marshalled into a sophisticated looking, swept up style and that alone changed the girl into a woman. The wide, clear, grey eyes looked at him warily as he came around the desk and stood in front of her, arms folded. The angry look of dismissal was no longer in his eyes at least, Trisa noted with relief.

'You still mad at me?' she asked him.

'I wasn't angry with you, Trisa,' he said softly. 'This was hurting,' he gestured to his wrist, 'and I was tired.'

She was glad to be back on the old footing with him for his recent coolness had been unbearable. Now she smiled and looked with frank admiration at a very smart, graceful Talbot. The black, high button vest showed off his straight, narrow waist and an expensive-looking, full-sleeved linen shirt and soft, highly polished boots made him look better than anything else that would be at her party.

'Where've you been all day?' she asked, inquisitively fingering the soft velvet stuff of his tie.

'I had some business to take care of in town for your father.'

'Did you get your bandage changed like Doc Jerome said?'

He nodded, showing her the clean white gauze under the sleeve of his shirt and she fingered that too, running her thumb over his wrist and the back of his hand.

'Did Louise put your hair up for you?' He put his hands on her shoulders and made her turn, while he inspected the intricate structure at the back. He could see the glint of many pins.

'Louise said she'd make a lady out of me if it killed her.'

'Just don't go near any magnets,' he

gravely warned her.

'I wanted to look nice tonight,' she shrugged and her unspoken 'for you' hung on the air between them.

'You look beautiful,' he said and hated himself for saying it, knowing she would take more out of it than some other girl used to easy compliments. She *was* beautiful and he had no right to tell her so.

Taken aback by his words, she watched with widened eyes as he took a small box from his shirt pocket and gave it to her, his birthday gift. Inside, a gold locket lay on a bed of red silk. Like Trisa's yellow dress, this was an heirloom too, a gift from his grand-mother on the day before he left for war. He explained this to Trisa as she lifted it from the box and held the heavy, expensive gold heart in her palm. She pictured his grandmother as frail, wispy-haired, taking his two strong hands in her gnarled, blue-veined old ones and imploring him to come home safe to her as she gave him her gift.

Talbot remembered her more accurately as a tall, straight, still-beautiful, very sophisticated Bostonite, in her early sixties then, wearing her most fashionable gown and an array of priceless jewellery. She had risen early to take breakfast with him before he left and had given him the locket then. It was the first gift her husband had ever given her and Nathan, out of all her grandchildren, was the one who most reminded her of her very much loved Nathaniel, for whom he was named. She felt somehow that his gift would protect the boy in what was to come for him.

'You know what this means to me,' she reminded him in her clipped, flat-vowelled Boston accent. 'So I don't want to hear of it turning up in a brothel, around some pretty harlot's neck.'

It had never left his person throughout the war years and it was a little scratched now, though still heavily beautiful. The gunsmith had cleaned it and tightened the clasp and had placed it in the little presentation box today.

He fastened it for her, facing her, his fingers so completely familiar with the clasp that he had no need to look and was able to concentrate instead on the delight in her eyes. For Trisa, it was as if he had given her part of himself.

'It looks much better on you,' he admitted with a smile. 'Happy birthday, Trisa.'

He saw her reaching up to kiss him and he bent to offer his cheek, but Trisa did not want anything so chaste. She wanted and found his lips, kissing him so hard he could feel her front teeth, her body stretching against him, two arms locked around his neck.

He disengaged in order to draw a ragged breath, shocked by his own body's treacherous response to her. Her innocent, untutored kiss seared him as much as Castle's red hot poker had done the other night. He spoke her name, hoarsely, and then showed her how, kissing her gently and slowly, parting her mouth a little to taste her with his tongue, lifting her against him. She smelt so young and fragrant. She tasted like everything he had ever wanted.

They separated at the same moment, Trisa's legs shaking, her hands gripping his arms. Talbot was coiled like a watch spring, the turbulence of desire and dismay darkening his eyes.

'You think I'm too young, don't you,' she said in a low, earnest voice, stroking his upper arms, as if to soothe him.

'Doctor Jerome gave me some whiskey the other night that was older than you,' he feebly joked.

'My mother was already married with a baby at my age,' she protested. Talbot shook his head and tried to turn but she held him fast.

'It's not that you're too young, Trisa, but that I'm just . . . wrong for you.'

'No,' she barely whispered it, afraid that for once in her life she might not have her own way. 'I love you, Nathan.'

Before he could reply, she reached up to him again, using the only weapon at her disposal, a sweet moist mouth that stifled his words and breath, silenced for a few precious moments all his objections.

She was a quick student. She knew now to part her lips and tentatively explore with her tongue, causing Talbot to make a sound she had never heard a man make before, and she held him fast with her arms around his waist, stroking his back, refusing to be put aside until a voice from the doorway made her turn in surprise.

'Well that's really touching, folks,' Murch said, as he lounged against the jamb, arms folded.

'Ray Murch, what do you think you're doing, just walking in — ?'

'All right, Trisa,' Talbot took her by the arm and guided her out of the room, past the leering Murch. He gave her a gentle push outside.

'I'll see you in a minute,' he said and he closed the door on her surprised face. He walked to the desk, lifted the money and began counting it out into the amused Murch's open hand.

'Got to give you credit for a fast worker, Talbot. Get the brother out of the way and then make a move on the sister.'

Murch never knew what hit him. One minute he was standing in front of Talbot, an ugly sneer on his face, the next he was on his rump on the floor, nursing a bloody nose.

'You bastard,' he swore.

Talbot flexed his hand and reached down, taking hold of Murch by the arm and jerking him to his feet. He picked up the fallen money and folded it, stuffing it into Murch's shirt pocket.

'You'd better get your facts straight before you open your big mouth a second time,' he said evenly. Murch drew his shirt sleeve across his nose and stared at the blood on it.

'You'll be sorry you ever did that, Talbot,' he said hotly. 'We're gonna fix you next time.'

'I know. You people have been promising to fix me for a while now. I'm not holding my breath.'

Murch wheeled and slammed out of the room and Talbot sank back against the edge of the desk. He didn't think Murch's threat was an empty one, but somehow it didn't seem to matter. All he could think about was how it had felt, just for a few minutes, to hold and kiss Trisa and hear her say, 'I love you, Nathan.'

He straightened his neckcloth, smoothed his hair back with his hand and turned for the door, ready to greet the party guests.

18

From the shadows, Murch watched the birthday party, his pale, almost colourless eyes following the dancing couples, his foot tapping to the tune the four-piece band were playing. He was as patient as a cat at a mouse hole, waiting for his chance to strike.

He saw Talbot dancing with Louise and then with the school teacher, Miss Carmody, who laughed and blushed like a young girl in his arms. Then he waltzed with the parson's wife, who had a tendency to lead but who thought Talbot the best dancer she had ever stood up with. He noticed that he avoided dancing with the birthday girl. And when he wasn't dancing, he mingled with the neighbours, making sure everybody had a drink or a partner or a plate in their hand.

Murch then turned his attention to

Saville. Tonight he was using a walking stick, determined not to be seen in his wheelchair but already his face was beginning to show signs of strain. He had been on the point of finding a chair for the rest of the evening when a young boy, who had been making himself useful fetching a lemonade for someone, ran up to him with a message from Max, asking him if he could come to the bunkhouse right away. Murch, who had sent the message, waited to make sure Saville was heading for the bunkhouse and then turned and disappeared into the night.

The bunkhouse was in darkness when Saville opened the door and stepped inside. The only illumination was from the lights in the yard but there was enough to let him walk along the row of beds, his injured right leg dragging badly now with tiredness. He was more than half-way along this part of the room, when he heard a slight sound behind him.

'Is that you, Max?' he asked, starting

to turn, always an awkward business with stick and disobliging knee. He knew nothing more as something hit him hard on the forehead and he went down like a sack of potatoes. Murch stood over the body of his ex-employer for a victorious moment, his fist still clenched around the leather sap he had used, and then dragged Saville up between the double row of beds till he was almost at the junction with the area the hands called the parlour. Then calmly and methodically he poured coal-oil from the stove over one of the beds and dropped a lighted match on it.

He left the way he had come in, by an open window on the side away from the busy yard. He retreated to the stables, to make sure his parting gift was properly appreciated and when he was sure the blaze was well and truly unstoppable, he left, for good this time.

But Saville's departure from the festivities had been noticed. Talbot was the one the boy had been fetching the lemonade for. He had decided, after his encounter with Murch that he ought to stay sober. Then he saw the boy speaking to Saville and pointing. Talbot was instantly on the alert. He followed his partner, watched him go into the darkened bunkhouse and waited in vain for him to come out.

After five minutes, he decided to risk Saville's anger and interrupt whatever was going on in there. He opened the door and walked into an inferno.

One entire section of the bunkhouse was aflame and the room was already filled with thick, oily, choking smoke. The fire had not travelled down the line of beds but had spread back into the parlour and if Saville had been in that area, he would have perished very quickly.

'Mr Saville,' Talbot called, dropping down at once to ground level where the air was almost breathable. Receiving no answer, he went forward on knees and elbows, his hands groping from side to side, feeling for human contact. He heard a groan and almost at the same time his fingers touched a boot heel. Without wasting precious time trying to find out how Saville was injured, Talbot began to drag him by the ankles back the way he had come. Blinded by his own tears, coughing and retching on the acrid smoke and seared by rippling waves of appalling, unbearable heat from the spreading and strengthening flames, he came close to giving up. But finally, after what seemed an age, he reached door. He dug down deep into reserves he didn't know he had and swung Saville up from the floor, over his shoulder and crashed out into the fresh air.

Outside, a rescue party had already begun forming up a bucket brigade. They had wrongly assumed that the bunkhouse was unoccupied. Talbot, overcome finally by the heat and smoke and exertion, sank to the ground, lowering Saville as gently as he could. The others came to his aid now, lifting Saville and carrying him to the house. Max helped Talbot away from the raging inferno that the bunkhouse had become, leaving the shocked, bewildered party guests and the crew to try bringing the blaze under control.

Talbot came to lying on the sofa in the parlour and at first lay still, too dizzy and nauseous to move. He had eaten a lungful of smoke and his throat felt like a piece of raw meat being dragged over broken glass with every breath he took. Louise was sitting on the edge of the sofa, her face drawn with shock and concern. She pushed his hair back from his dirty forehead and applied a cold cloth to it.

'Lie still, honey,' she gently advised him, raising his head a little to give him a drink of water.

'Where's Trisa?' he asked hoarsely.

'With her father.'

'And Max?

'He went back out to help with the fire. The wind's shifted. He's afraid it might spread.'

'Is Mr Saville all right?'

'Doc Jerome just arrived. He's in

there with him. Now you just lie still and stop worrying about everybody else.'

Ignoring her, he started to rise and experienced such a headache that he could not prevent an overwhelming rush of nausea, and twisted on to his side in order to be sick. Louise had anticipated him and caught most of it in her bowl of bathing water. He lay back very slowly, his colour, under the soot and smoke, turning an alarming grey. Louise applied her cloth to his forehead again and seeing that he was for the moment prepared to lie still, eyes closed, got up to fetch Jerome to see to him.

In Gregory Saville's bedroom, the patient was being difficult. Saville had not ingested as much smoke as Talbot and the blow to the head had only stunned him. He was already trying to get up.

'In God's name, David, I'm all right. My whole ranch is about to go up in flames and you want me to take to my bed?'

'Your ranch is not in flames, Greg, just the bunkhouse. And there are at least sixty people out there helping put it out.'

The doctor turned as Louise came on the scene and gave his arm a gentle tug.

'Come and take a look at Nathan, would you? I don't like his colour and he's just been terrible sick.'

'What's the matter with him?' Saville demanded, since he had not been told who had pulled him out of the burning bunkhouse.

'It was Nathan who found you, Daddy,' Trisa explained.

'Pulled you out of it,' Jerome said, interestedly watching Saville's expression of dismay. He did not want to be in Talbot's debt. Anyone but Talbot.

'You'd better go and see to him, David,' he said grudgingly. But Talbot was gone. He was out in the yard, helping direct the firefighters, the soldier in him emerging with a vengeance, the ragged, disorganized party of volunteers suddenly finding themselves marshalled into an efficient team.

Saville was allowed to observe from the veranda, but no further, contradictory emotions and thoughts animating his face.

There was anger firstly that again someone had tried to kill him, relief that they had failed, disappointment that it was Talbot who had saved him and to whom he was now three times indebted. He watched him now and felt a grudging stab of admiration which did not lessen through that long night of smoke and heat as his good friends and neighbours fought to quell the fire. He knew that if it were Howard giving out the orders there would be chaos in minutes and they'd have been ready to lynch him before daybreak. But by the time the bunkhouse was reduced to carbon, Nathan Talbot had every man, woman and child with him, heart and soul. You couldn't buy that quality.

And it was difficult to believe that a

man who had those qualities could be all the things Howard had said in his letters, spiteful, jealous, vindictive, petty and universally despised. As the dawn arrived that morning, Gregory Saville was forced to confront a painful truth.

Nathan Talbot was not the man Howard had so meticulously described in his letters home. No, he was something quite different. He was hard-working, good-humoured, patient, generous, intelligent and self-effacing. He had shown physical courage on several occasions and tonight he had nearly lost his own life in trying to save Saville.

Why had Howard lied? Saville knew why. Perhaps he had always known the truth, but he aged a dozen years that night, finally acknowledging that the man Howard had described in his letters was pretty much himself.

Whatever had happened at Cherry Bridge had not been Talbot's doing. Saville was pretty near sure of that, a terrible accident possibly but certainly not deliberate. This man would have moved heaven and earth to save the men on that bridge.

Saville made up his mind then and there to tell Talbot that he no longer held him responsible for his son's death, but it would keep for another day.

Earlier he had watched Talbot already cutting a deal with Mr Fraser, who owned the lumber yard, for wood to rebuild the bunkhouse and then taking a rough inventory from the crew of what they had lost so that it could be replaced, scribbling details on a torn scrap of paper, making a joke with Tom Hobb about his stash of picture postcards, mainly of dancing girls, being lost for ever. And in fact Tom's pictures were about the only personal items lost that night, apart from some gear and clothing, because the policy at the ranch was that valuables of any kind were kept in the safe up at the house. Because no matter how good a berth the Saville ranch was, a bunkhouse full of men, sometimes complete strangers, was no place to leave a gold watch.

The last of Saville's neighbours had gone home when Talbot and Max and Trisa came towards the house, faces smoke-blackened, hair dirty, party clothes water stained and ruined, but everybody cheerful, making jokes.

As Talbot came up the steps to the veranda, Saville caught his eye. They looked at one another and Saville sensed that Talbot didn't want him to even mention what had happened in the bunkhouse, no thanks, no gratitude. So he said nothing. He nodded his head, no more than a quarter-inch, then turned and led everybody inside to the kitchen.

'Hot food this way,' he told them. 'Breakfast for everybody.' He paused to look back at his small family. Trisa in her mother's soot-streaked party dress, her carefully constructed hair-do curling limp around her neck; Louise, who had donned her apron and had been feeding people all night; Max with a scorched brow and a grin and Talbot who also looked slightly singed. Doc Jerome stood to one side of Talbot, in shirtsleeves, having tended various minor ailments through the night, now just about ready to do battle with his original patients, to try to get both Saville and Talbot to rest for a while.

Saville tried to smile at them, at the people who mattered most in the world to him. He cleared his throat and tried to speak, coughed and tried again and at last said, 'Looks like the Saville ranch lives to fight another day.'

19

It would have made no difference to Talbot to know that Saville had suffered a radical change of heart towards him. He knew that his hours on this ranch were numbered, that Murch was only waiting his chance to make one final bit of mischief.

He started getting things into order, leaving everything straight for Saville, working like a demon to finish all that he had undertaken. The others watched him worriedly, unable to comprehend his punishing schedule, unable to persuade him that it was not necessary to drive himself so hard, not necessary to kill himself for the Saville ranch. But Talbot was like a man with a death sentence hanging over him. He especially avoided Trisa, wanting no more of those scenes in the library. That would be hard enough to put behind him without encouraging more.

Two weeks after the fire he returned late one evening after a long, gruelling day in the saddle, with every intention of ending his partnership with Saville that very night.

He circled around the skeleton of the new bunkhouse and dismounted with evident weariness close to one of the corrals. As his hands fumbled tiredly for the girth strap, a boot crunched on the dry ground beside him and Max moved in, putting Talbot to one side while he took over the business of stripping saddle and gear.

'Thanks, Max,' Talbot said gratefully and he lifted his hat and rubbed the raw area of forehead where the sweat band had chafed. Max worked in silence for a while, ignoring Talbot, but when he was ready to lead the horse away he turned, and his eyes were curiously hard and watchful.

'You'd better get cleaned up. They're all wonderin' where you got to, especially Trisa.'

'I didn't expect to be so late. Had to take care of some things in Caldwell.'

'Did you see your friend Ray Murch?'

Talbot took an indecisive, half-step towards the foreman.

'What do you mean?'

'I was just asking who you saw in town is all,' Max said with a slight shrug. An icy stillness came over Talbot. He stared at the ranch foreman in silence, just waiting for the rest of it.

'Or was it your other friend, Doc Jerome? Was he the one spoke up for you at your trial, tried to get you off for murdering all those men on that bridge? Ray Murch told me pretty much the whole story, Nate. I just wish you'd had the guts to tell me yourself. I thought we were friends.'

When he had delivered his final shaft, Max watched to see its effect on Talbot. His face wore the same expression of futility it had borne that hot, close, thundery day, the day they tried him, though this time he did not twist and

195

fall, limp in the mud. This time he began walking away under his own power.

Max did not let him walk far before he caught his arm and turned him around.

'So that's why you let Murch walk that night. And that's why you've been working like a maniac, trying to get all your little jobs finished before Murch opened his big mouth. How could you come here, Nate? Letting those people get to like you, get to trust you and all the time — '

'I didn't know this was the Saville ranch, not till you told me. I tried to leave as soon as I came to that night. You stopped me.'

'You didn't have to stay.'

'I just wanted to help. I thought I could help.'

Max released Talbot's arm. His expression was one of bewildered anger rather than hatred or accusation.

'Well, I suppose you have. You saved Trisa's life, I guess. And you saved the boss from losing the ranch and being spit-roasted in the bunkhouse. In my book that evens the score,' Max admitted, though grudgingly. 'What's your side of it anyway? What really did happen on that bridge?'

Talbot unwillingly dragged his mind back to the rain and mud and Cherry Bridge. He could still smell the mud. He could still feel the pulse of fever in his head. A single bead of sweat began to wind down his check, curving in towards his mouth. He brushed it away with his hand as he relived those last terrible minutes for probably the thousandth time.

'I'd been ill. I refused to turn command over to someone else and I . . . made a mistake. I lit the fuse to blow the bridge too soon.'

Max shook his head. He thought it was a rotten shame.

'Have you told them, Louise and Trisa and the others?' he asked in a neutral tone, but dreading the answer. The foreman would never forget meeting Murch in Caldwell and having to listen to the poison he had spilled while Max tried to control an impulse to kill the little creep. But he had been alone, and Murch had company, two hefty, hard-eyed bodyguards.

'I'm not playing that bastard's dirty game. You know, he all but admitted torching the bunkhouse. But it's all finished for you here, Nate. I told you we should have done something about him that night.'

'It doesn't matter, Max. I came home tonight to tell the boss I was quitting anyway.'

'What will you do? Where will you go?' Max asked. Talbot shook his head bleakly. For some reason today was chosen as the day when his life was to be delivered up to him in ruins, the life it really was, despite his own recent efforts to paper over the cracks.

'Stay with David Jerome for a few days maybe, till I decide. I guess I better go in and see about dissolving the partnership.'

He had gone as far as the front porch when a word from Max stopped him in his tracks. Most of the crew, led by Jack Spinner, who had known Howard Saville when he was a boy, were heading towards him, a hostile tide of angry men with bunched fists. Spinner gave a signal and before Max could intervene, they moved in on Talbot and hustled him towards the barn.

Max quickly tethered Talbot's horse and sprinted after them but the crew were reluctant to let him through. He had to force his way to the front. Talbot was being held against the barn wall. His hat was gone and his waistcoat forcibly undone, half the buttons torn loose, his shirt collar was torn, his mouth bleeding.

'Let him go,' Max demanded.

'Get lost if you're squeamish, Ryan. We're not through yet.'

Without a word, the foreman turned, shouldering his way through the press of bodies and headed for the ranch house at a run, while they took Talbot into the barn to finish him off, shutting but not barring the door to conduct their bloody retribution in private.

Max burst into the kitchen, startling its occupants, Louise by the stove, worrying over Talbot's dried up supper, Trisa at the table listening to her father read out something in the newspaper. Max firmly put Louise to one side in order to reach for the shotgun on the wall, where it had been kept handy in earlier days, tore open a drawer in search of shells and then another till he found them and without a word, ignoring their shouted questions, turned and ran back the way he had come.

It took only a couple of seconds for them to follow him, their shock and bewilderment intensifying when they saw him kick the barn door open, pausing only to load the shotgun.

Trisa raced past him and got there first, taking in the scene with one shocked sweep of the eyes, a solitary lantern casting a pool of light on crew and victim. She could make no sense of it. Her father's crew were holding Nathan by the arms, so tightly his mouth was stretched with pain. There was blood on his face and down his shirt front and one of the hands was about to punch him again, his bunched knuckles drawn back for the blow.

'Let him go,' she screamed at them, facing up to the biggest of them, trying to push him back.

'Get her out of here,' Jack Spinner barked and two of the crew took her arms and started to eject her from the barn. Talbot struggled now. Before, he had let them do what they liked to him, not caring, but when he saw them lay hands on Trisa, roughly turning her, dragging her away, he was incensed.

He tore loose, cut two of them down with a speed and strength that surprised and angered them, his fists breaking at least one nose and a couple of ribs, decking a third man and winding a fourth before a rifle stock took him out of it. He fell, stunned, to the floor and was brutally dragged back to his feet and held once again. After this mayhem, Trisa's protests grew louder.

'What has he done for you to hold him like that? Nathan, what's happening?'

'He killed your brother,' somebody told her brutally. 'Now if you want something done about it, go on back to the house.'

'Howard was killed in the war,' she contradicted angrily, but she was close to tears by this time, her heart pounding with fear.

'This is Captain Talbot, Trisa,' Spinner told her, taking her by the arm and shoving her up closer to Talbot. Somebody jerked his lolling head back by the hair so that his eyes could painfully focus on the dead man's sister. 'Captain Talbot blew Howie to bits on Cherry Bridge. Ask your pa if you don't believe us.'

Standing back slightly, Louise suddenly had a glimpse of the truth.

'Come on, honey,' she said to Trisa

and took her arm. Trisa pulled free.

'No, they're lying,' she cried, turning to Talbot with an expression on her face that tore the heart from him.

'Trisa . . . go back to the house,' he begged her quietly. She saw that though he looked the same, except for a little blood and his clothing disordered, there was a broken look in his eyes. At that moment, Greg Saville came to stand beside his daughter, moving her gently to one side as he faced the mob ranged around Nathan Talbot. Leaning quite heavily still on his walking cane, he looked into each face, into each eye until he had their attention.

'All right, you've had your fun. This ends here and now. As for you, Spinner, you're fired.'

Jack Spinner looked almost comically aggrieved at this, his jaw working as if he were chewing on his fury.

'Well, it's a sad day, when a man won't even stand up for his own son's memory. We came here tonight to put it right for Howie but you — '

'I don't need the likes of you to defend my family's honour,' Saville replied calmly. 'Pack your gear and get out. Any of the rest of you feels the same way, your wages are in my office.'

The others, recognizing a good berth when they had found one, murmured to one another, shuffled their feet awkwardly and began to drift away, leaving Spinner and one other man, Archie Forrest. Spinner continued his staring contest with Saville and then with a nod to the other man, turned and left. As he swung out through the barn door, Max lowered the shotgun and moved forward to stand beside Saville and the two women.

And still Trisa stared at him, wanting him to put it all back the way it was, to make it all right. At least now she understood her father's attitude to Talbot these last weeks, his coldness and dislike. He had known all along and had been unable to hide his hatred for the man who killed his only son.

She acquired ten years maturity that

night, standing in the dimly lit barn, looking at the man she had wanted more than breath. And Talbot painfully watched the years creep into those wide, grey eyes and he would have given anything to spare her.

'Just tell me it's not true and I'll believe you,' she said, stepping up to him, searching his face for a reprieve. He was silent, unable to speak, and it was Max who finally spoke.

'It was just an accident, Trisa. He was sick and didn't know what he was doing. And now he's leaving. Come on, Nate.'

Blindly, without looking directly at anyone, Talbot followed Max up to the house and into the front hallway.

He looked about him at the familiar things in the house, things he had grown accustomed to seeing and touching every day. He realized with a start that he had come to think of this long, cool hacienda as home. Talbot drew in a deep breath. It tasted of warm, fresh bread, coffee and bougainvillea, the essence of the Saville home. The thought of leaving it, leaving Trisa and Louise and Max and even Greg Saville and returning to his lonely, self-inflicted isolation was unbearable.

Max picked a bit of straw from his shirt and then pressed his own clean handkerchief to Talbot's mouth.

'You're bleeding,' he said.

'I'll go up and pack.'

'Why not wait until morning?'

'No. It's best if I leave tonight. Will you drive me to town? I'll leave the mare here.'

Max was about to argue, then sighed and shrugged.

'I'd have given anything to have spared her from all that,' Talbot said and Max nodded.

'I know.'

He climbed the stairs slowly, dragging his feet. He should have been glad that it was all over at last, that he had a good excuse to leave, but he felt desolate, incredibly sad that the people he had come to care for should suddenly feel such contempt and hatred for him.

He opened the door of his own room and walked inside and instantly he knew that he was not alone. The memory of the attack in the barn was too fresh in his mind for him not to react and he ducked, to the right, but was struck anyway by a pounding fist that caught him on the back of the neck and stunned him. He put out a hand to save himself but almost immediately another blow slammed him into the bedroom wall, his forehead splitting against the tough plaster surface.

As he slid, lifeless, to a sitting position on the floor, his attacker bent over and gagged him, bound his wrists and ankles and lifted him over one shoulder with athletic ease. Talbot's head swung in a brief pendulum and drops of blood from his forehead made a wide circle on the floor, before he was lowered from the window on to the roof of the back porch and then down into the darkened yard. His abductor adjusted Talbot's unconscious body across his shoulder and then slipped away into the night.

Downstairs, Max and Louise had wound up in the kitchen, drinking coffee and discussing the events of the last half-hour. Trisa and her father were in the study, where, occasionally, raised voices could be heard. Unlike the loyal Saville crew Louise had never been one of Howard's biggest fans, and she liked Nathan too much to hate him.

'It's just a pity Trisa didn't know her brother as well as I did,' Louise remarked. Max hadn't known Howard, having come to the ranch after his own military service. Now he looked keenly at Louise, the love of his life, even though he hadn't gotten round to telling her yet, and realized there were things about her he didn't know either.

'After he died, I didn't think there was any point in taking away her illusions. Let her think the best of him, I used to say to myself, keep your mouth shut when she talks about her brave, wonderful big brother. But when I saw the look on her face tonight in the barn, when Jack Spinner told everybody, I wished I'd told her every sordid detail, every rotten contemptible thing he ever did.'

Max stared at his normally gentle, sweet Louise and wondered just what exactly Howard Saville had done or tried to do to her. She was a handsome woman. She would have been even more attractive when Howard was living on the ranch. Then she smiled at him to let him see that whatever it was, she had survived it and he smiled back at her.

'I wish I hadn't listened to Nathan the night of Trisa's party,' he repeated for the second time that night. 'None of this would've happened if we had done what I wanted to do with that miserable little bastard Murch.'

'But what's it all about, Max? Why would Murch do those things? How did he know about Nathan?'

Max had been asking himself the

same questions for weeks now but he was no nearer a solution. And now he would have to try to figure it out alone, without Talbot.

'Where is he anyway? He said he'd be ten minutes.'

Talbot was not in his room, Max found when he went to check. His clothes were still either hanging tidily in the closet or folded neatly in the drawers of the bureau, his grip still where it had been stowed the night he arrived, in a corner behind a chair. His hat lay tilted against the foot of the bed and the window was wide open, the drapes stirring gently in the faintest of breezes. Max noted all of this with one sweep of his eyes. Now he took a longer look.

There was a drying smear of blood on the wall behind the door, drops of it on the floor and window ledge. And a smell in the room. Max inhaled and frowned. It was faintly spicy, faintly animal.

It was rarely enough that Max Ryan

knew fear, but he knew it now, for Talbot, as he crossed the room and leaned out of the window, looking down on to the quiet, darker side of the house. Below, on the roof of the back porch, a shingle that had been slowly sliding down since being stepped on by Talbot's attacker, reached the edge of the roof and fell with a metallic clatter.

'God help you, Nathan,' Max breathed and he closed the window and turned to hurry downstairs.

20

The Fletcher mining camp had been played out and abandoned forty years ago, the shacks and storage buildings left to weather and decay, the mining equipment that couldn't be carried away allowed to rust and petrify. Situated in a rocky outcrop a few miles adrift of Saville's southernmost boundary, it was as secure as a fortress, with direct access only through a narrow, dog-leg ravine.

The men who had been hired to harry Saville had moved in, brought supplies and women, posted a guard and made regular forays on to Saville property to do what their paymaster bade them. They were a mixed bunch of wanted men, Conrad and Baker, Castle and Billy among them and a few others, deserters and misfits, the godless and godforsaken of every description. They came out to watch now as Gila rode down into the middle of the camp, leading a walking man, his wrists bound in front of him.

Talbot had been walking since daybreak. He had come to after being abducted to find himself facing an Indian of powerful physique, tawny and handsome, over six foot of sinew, and muscle, his body pocked and scarred by a life of violence and conflict. He wore a blue Union army shirt with the sleeves torn off at the shoulder, a leather kilt and soft, good quality brown leather boots. His black hair was cropped short except for a section that had been left to grow just behind his left ear and which had been braided and interwoven with beads and coloured threads.

'I guess you must be, Gila,' Talbot said and Gila nodded, recognizing his own name.

'Yes, I am Gila, and I am going to skin you alive and make you eat your own manhood for what you have done to my woman,' he said in his own tongue and then he bound Talbot and jerked him to his feet and made him walk, a rope looped around his wrists.

Talbot tried to leave a trail of breadcrumbs, in the hope that Max or somebody might follow him, a button here, a scrap of paper under a stone there, a groove pointing the way scraped into the dust when Gila wasn't looking, but now as he looked around at the faces watching him, he knew no one was going to rescue him from here.

Gila had his own little cadre of men, two brothers and a cousin. They had been with him when he had been led to the shallow grave where his wife lay. Traditionally, in Gila's tribe, women were accorded no special funeral rights, but this woman was different. They had helped him bury her with all the ceremony and dignity usually reserved for a great warrior, and now they looked at the man they had been told had killed her. One of them spat in Talbot's face, the other brought his knife up to his eye and would have sliced it open but Gila stopped him.

'Later,' he told them.

Gila twisted the rope connected to Talbot's wrists and yanked him hard towards one of the shacks.

Inside a man sat at a table playing strip poker with two girls. One of the girls was down to her drawers and chemise. The other was wearing the man's hat and vest. Gila spoke to him in Spanish and the man stood up and came to the door to listen and nod to what he had to say. Gila spoke again, took one last long look at Talbot and then left.

'My lieutenant has other business,' he explained. 'But he'll be back to take care of you later. You must be Captain Talbot. My name is Francisco.' He held out a hand, an affable smile on his face. He was a fairly short man, stocky and dark, with golden mountain-lion eyes and brutal smallpox scarring on his cheeks. Talbot held out his bound wrists, ruefully indicating his inability to shake hands. Francisco produced a knife and cut the bindings, allowing Talbot to peel the thin hide away from his flesh.

'Thanks.'

'Would you like anything? I have tequila and brandy.'

'Just water.' Francisco signalled to one of the girls and she got up with bad grace, slouching across the floor in dirty, bare feet to the water pail and brought a jugful. She was drenched in cheap perfume and her chemise was unlaced at the front, revealing very young and very slight brown breasts. She was just a child, no more than fifteen or sixteen. Talbot thanked her for the water and something in his look made her draw her clothes together and with a nod to her even younger friend, the two of them left. Talbot tried to drink the water slowly, eyes closed, body quivering slightly as he slaked his thirst.

'He knows how to make a man suffer,' Francisco observed. 'So, you're the famous Captain Talbot. And you've graduated from killing soldiers to killing women.'

Talbot had nurtured a pathetic hope that he had been kidnapped because he worked for Saville, or as just another part of the dirty campaign against the ranch, but his worst fear, that Gila blamed him for the girl's death, had just been confirmed.

'I didn't kill her,' Talbot said flatly.

'All right,' Francisco said easily. 'Come and sit and tell me what happened.'

Talbot was glad of a seat. He lowered himself slowly on to a rickety chair at the table and then pretended to inspect his recently burned wrist. Gila's binding had bit deep into it but it was the look in the other man's eyes that troubled him, not the raw wound on his wrist. Francisco knew that he hadn't killed the girl. Raising his eyes, he watched the other man pour himself some brandy, smiling as he corked the bottle and then raised the dirty glass to his mouth.

'Me and my foreman found and buried her. She'd been stabbed and raped, left for dead in the sun. She tried to tell us who it was but we couldn't make her out.'

'Even if that's true, I couldn't change Gila's mind. I've got a certain hold over him but it's a delicate thing and I wouldn't ruin a good relationship to save you.'

'It suits your purpose to let him murder me, doesn't it,' Talbot said, with a flash of insight.

'I haven't any instructions regarding you, only Saville.'

'Instructions from whom?'

Francisco leaned forward with an appreciative smile.

'You don't talk like anybody I ever met before. You must've got a pretty good education, went to all the good schools, huh?'

Talbot smiled despite himself, to hear his education being discussed in this filthy, disgusting camp.

'I went to all the best schools. You see where it's got me.'

Talbot took another pull from the water jug, dried his mouth with his arm then allowed the back of the chair to take the weight of his back. Since Francisco was still playing the genial host, he asked another question.

'Why does Gila think I killed the woman?'

'Somebody told him, somebody he trusts.'

'Who?'

Francisco considered for a while. He lit a fresh cigar and the cheap tarry odour of it, mingling with the smoke of the fire over which a pot of stew was simmering and the sweet and sweaty odours of the women drifted over Talbot, mingling with the sharp odour of his own body, and he wondered, for the hundredth time, how he had come to be here at all.

'I don't think it makes any difference if you know. It was Ray Murch who told him,' Francisco said and Talbot shut his eyes and nodded, laughing softly to himself.

'I should've listened to you, Max,' he murmured to himself.

They tied Talbot between two poles in the middle of the camp where he remained all day, until one of the men from the livery barn put in an appearance. It was Baker. He leaned his ugly face in close and told Talbot what he was going to do to Trisa next time he had her pinned on the ground. White hot rage lanced through Talbot, his body jerking towards the big man so hard he nearly dislocated his shoulder. Baker laughed, made a fist, held it under Talbot's nose to let him see what was coming and then punched him hard under the ribs with it. He watched Talbot struggle for air for a minute or two then strolled away.

Along towards evening, Talbot sensed a change in the air. It was twilight now but there was a deeper darkness in the sky and he lifted his head and saw those familiar black rollers heading in across the darkening sky, but this time they stayed and unloaded their goods on the thirsty land. The downpour came and he lowered his head to wait it out, alone in the centre of the camp now. Six hours later, several hundred gallons later, he was still there, hanging by the wrists and not giving a damn about anything.

Gila came out of the dark so suddenly that Talbot visibly started. His eyes were wild, he had been drinking and he was in a mood to put an end to things between himself and Talbot. But the storm had put paid to that.

He drew his knife and sliced the thongs at Talbot's wrists. The dull weight of his arms was too much for him and he sagged to his knees with a hoarse cry of relief. Gila stood over him for fully a minute, his face working, the desire to simply slit Talbot's craven throat so powerful he almost gave in to it. Then, with a muttered curse under his breath, he roughly pulled Talbot's arms behind him, securing him again with fresh bindings, hoisted him to his feet and half carried him to Francisco's shack, which he opened by kicking the door back. Francisco shouted a protest, from the depths of the blanket he and one of his young mistresses were wrapped in. Gila snarled back at him and dropped Talbot in a corner.

Talbot fell on a fairly soft woven rug, landing on his face. Gila kicked him, walked away a few steps, came back and kicked him again, and then slammed out of the shack. In the low cot in the corner, the girl looked at Francisco, who shrugged and turned over to go back to sleep. She, the child of the water jug, slipped out of bed and fetched a blanket for Talbot and crouching, covered him with it. She wanted to untie him but knew she did not dare. She watched him for a moment, glimpsing suddenly a different sort of man, saw a different life from the one she lived. She stroked his hair off his forehead and then reluctantly crept back into bed with her protector, a man who routinely stole, and lied and cheated and murdered and who would pass her on to one of his subordinates when he grew tired of her. She turned her back on him so that she could lie in the flickering light of the low burning fire and watch the other man till she slept.

Talbot watched her too, grateful for her small act of kindness, his cheek pressed into the warm stuff of the blanket she had thrown over him. A blissful, aching tiredness swamped him. He felt his body start to glow with the insulated heat of the place and in a very short time he had drifted into an exhausted sleep. In the morning they found him in the first stages of fever.

Gila came at first light, took a look at him and realized that he would have to postpone his much sought after revenge until Talbot was at least coherent. He spoke to Francisco for a few minutes then helped himself to some of the bacon frying in the pan over the fire, wrapped it in a hunk of bread and left.

Francisco conducted his business in the shack just as usual all that next day, largely ignoring the sick man in the corner. His two young female friends gave Talbot water and ran a dirty cloth over his brow once in a while which was more nursing than he might otherwise have expected. Talbot, at the height of his fever, knew only Cherry Bridge and then in more lucid moments, he heard snatches of conversation, Francisco speaking to someone, their voices low and confidential.

'We've been kicking our heels in this godforsaken hole for months, waiting for your boss to get back and give us the rest of our money. We're not sticking around here any longer. The US marshal is looking for Castle. Him and Billy have already gone and Conrad with them. You tell him. We get our money by Friday or he can take care of Saville with his own lily white hands.'

'He knows, Frankie. He had business elsewhere, couldn't be helped. He'll be back Tuesday. I'm to meet him off the last train Tuesday night and he'll have the rest of your gold by Friday, no problem. Everybody gets paid and you can finish the job.' Talbot recognized the speaker. It was Murch.

'If you're not here by sunup Saturday, we're leaving,' Francisco persisted stubbornly. Murch turned on him, his collar suddenly too tight around his thick, bull neck, his face mottled, ugly with fury.

'You've all but bled my boss dry already and what have you done, tinkered at the edges, got nowhere. You'd better finish this job, Frankie, or so help me God, you'll be sorry.'

Francisco's eyes had turned hot with responding anger, but he decided to cool things down. He gave a rueful shrug and reached for the brandy bottle, offering it to Murch.

'Calmly, my friend. We will do all you ask with pleasure. It's just that it's getting too hot for us here and Gila is like a caged animal, thanks to you. Why did you have to go and kill the Lark?' Francisco asked then.

'How do you know?' the other man demanded.

'I'm not stupid. He would no more hurt a woman than fly in the air,' Francisco said, jerking a thumb at Talbot. 'And Gila isn't stupid either. If he finds out, you'll pray for a gun to blow your own brains out.'

'And are you going to tell him? So what if I had a little fun with her. What the hell Frankie, she was just a half-breed Indian whore. I took her where I knew Talbot and Ryan would be riding and I waited till they were pretty close, then I killed her. I knew they would find her and that Gila would blame them, maybe kill both of them. I thought it would save us a lot of trouble if it happened that way.'

'Sure, Ray. You've always got everybody's best interests at heart. That's why you killed Jud Willis too, huh? Except you forgot one small detail. Willis was our second man inside the ranch. It wasn't up to you to decide to kill him,' Francisco sneered.

226

'He stuck his nose in my business, Frankie. He thought he could make a little sideline out of me but he found out different,'

'What kind of a sideline?'

'He was going to go to Talbot to tell him about the girl if I didn't give him a bigger cut. I found him digging around in my stuff that I had stashed in the hayloft, so I took care of him. End of story.'

'And that's another thing. Your boss didn't want anything to happen to him,' Francisco jerked his chin in Talbot's direction. Murch put his head on one side as he looked at Talbot, lying on the cot, his eyes bright with fever.

'I don't think the boss will mind that much.'

'I know you,' Talbot murmured aloud and Murch came and stood over him.

'And I know you, Captain. Our big war hero. And you're going to take my medicine, aren't you. Gila's going to skin you alive. You should have left her on the ground like Max told you to.'

'Leave him alone,' one of the girls said, squaring up to Murch. He looked at her with eyes that reminded her of a lizard and she spat at the ground between his feet.

'Don't start anything in here,' Francisco warned and after a staring contest they both backed down, Murch laughing his high-pitched laugh and the girl retreating to sit with her friend in the corner. Francisco and Murch drifted outside then, leaving Talbot to wonder incoherently who Murch's boss could be and why they had been told to lay off where he was concerned.

'Doesn't make any sense,' he murmured, and the girl came to sit beside him, blotting the burning sweat from his face, murmuring to him in Spanish, wishing she knew a way to help.

In the evening, a card game in one of the other shacks kept Francisco from her bed and the girl, Marguerita, drifted outside for a breath of air. Looking up at the sky she saw that there was more rain on the way, low, swollen, inky clouds piling up. She wandered around the back of the shack, where there was a latrine of sorts and was about to relieve herself when a big, meaty fist, callused and powerful, clamped over her mouth, an arm tightened around her waist and Max Ryan whispered in her ear.

'Don't scream and I won't hurt you.'

21

Talbot lingered on the edge of oblivion for two more days before returning like a prodigal to the light of day, Cherry Bridge blown up one last time. The explosion ripped through the confines of his brain for the thousandth time since it had actually happened and his body jerked, arms raised over his face. As Talbot lay in a puddle of his own cold sweat, hardly breathing, waiting for the tension to ease, two strong hands gripped his wrists and firmly lowered them.

'All right now?' a low voice asked and Talbot turned his head on the damp pillow to see who had spoken and recognized the doctor. He was in Doctor Jerome's house in Caldwell, in one of the doctor's spare bedrooms, though he could not remember how he had come to be here. All that had existed for him was that rain-sodden camp and the compressed events of that final week at Cherry Bridge.

'What time is it? How long have I been here?' he asked as the doctor released his wrists. His voice sounded hoarse with ill-usage. He knew that when he was fevered he talked incessantly and sometimes quite lucidly.

'It's evening, a little after eight. You've been here for two days. I sent Max home a few minutes ago,' Jerome said and he rubbed both hands over his face with tiredness, as if he could wash away the weariness and worry of the last few days.

'Max?'

'He brought you home, Nathan, trailed you and Gila and brought you out of that mining camp.'

A memory dislodged itself from the bed of Talbot's sub-conscious and began to surface, but he was too tired, his thoughts too confused to separate it from all the other driftwood. He struggled with it for a minute and then let his head fall back on the pillow.

'It rained. I remember that,' he murmured.

'Nearly two days of it. At least one of Greg Saville's problems solved.'

Jerome watched him quietly for a few minutes. They had both been through hell these past two days, this bout probably worse than any Talbot had endured so far. Jerome wondered what would happen when the next bout came and there was nobody there to pull him out the other end.

'Are you hungry?' he enquired and Talbot shook his head.

'No.'

'Just tired, huh?'

'How could you tell?' he asked with a ghost of a smile.

'You've been all the way back to the war on foot these past couple of days. Bound to be tired.'

The memory flickered against the back of his vision again and he frowned with concentration.

'I've been running off at the mouth, I suppose.'

'And then some. You cursed Sergeant Lyons a fair bit, not to mention my own good self, then you got yourself blown up once or twice.'

'Nothing else?' He sounded anxious and Jerome looked at him more closely.

'Just the damn bridge, Nathan, over and over. I feel as if I never left the place. I want you to forget it for a while and get some real sleep now, huh? And then some food.'

Talbot felt the sheets being arranged tightly about his person and then the lamp was turned out completely. Jerome hovered for a minute, wondering whether to remain, but Talbot was over the worst and the promise of another working day and his own fatigue finally won out. He turned for the door, but paused, his hand on the handle.

'You just kept asking the time, and what day it was, over and over.'

'I did?'

'As though you had an appointment or something. Just the fever talking I expect. Anyway, goodnight, Nathan. If you need anything, just sing out. I'm right next door and my housekeeper and her husband are in the room above you.'

'Thanks, David, for everything. Goodnight.' He was asleep before Jerome closed the bedroom door. He slept like a dead man for the rest of the night and all of the following day.

22

With his business at the lumber yard completed, Max stopped by to visit with Talbot for a little while, pausing at the kitchen to say hello to Doctor Jerome's housekeeper, Mrs Addie. She told him the doctor had gone out earlier in the evening.

In Talbot's bedroom the bed was empty, though still warm. Max, fearing the return of Gila or worse, looked out of the window and saw a familiar figure heading for the stable.

'What the hell — ' he murmured and, turning, left the room and hurried downstairs.

When he entered the stable, he saw Talbot engrossed in the business of saddling his own horse. Max walked up to him and stood off to one side, watching curiously. Talbot noted his presence but ignored him, for his whole attention was taken up with the girth strap, which was defying all his efforts to tighten it.

'Where do you think you're going?' Max asked him. Talbot continued to work in silence, his throbbing head lowered to the task in hand. 'It's late, Nate. Can't it wait till morning? Then I'll take you wherever you want to go.'

Eventually he looked up at Max with a troubled expression on his face, his eyes still a little cloudy with fever, his face and throat slick with sweat.

'I don't think this will keep till morning,' he said.

'What won't?'

'I have to get to the railroad station before seven o'clock. Is there still time?' he asked distractedly, pressing a thumb and forefinger into his waistcoat pocket for his watch, which was not there, was in fact still lying on the dresser in his bedroom at the ranch. No one had thought to bring it to him yet. He laid the flat of his hand against Max's vest pocket and with unaccustomed clumsiness pulled out the foreman's old battered timepiece. He sprung the cover but the numbers meant nothing to his exhausted brain.

'I have to be at the railroad station at seven.'

'I know. You told me that, Nate.' Max said gently, taking his father's watch out of Talbot's hand and returning it to his pocket. 'Can you give me a little hint here as to why you have to be at the railroad at seven?'

Talbot tried to remember what had driven him out of bed half an hour ago. In fact it had been the doctor's wall clock chiming six o'clock that had jolted him awake with an urgency he could not explain.

'Is it really that important?' Max asked him, as he observed how exhausted Talbot was just staying on his feet.

'I don't know. I think it might be. Something . . . I overheard something at the mining camp. Will you help me,

Max? I have to go.'

Max shook his head but over the last weeks he had come to recognize that Nathan Talbot was that rare thing, a cast-iron certainty, and even though he was evidently still a very sick man and perhaps not altogether right in his head, Max was sure that if he needed to be at the railroad station by seven then there had to be a good reason.

'All right, Nathan, but not on horseback.'

He borrowed a buggy at the livery stable and they drove out of the yard and on to the road to Osborne. The cool air on his face revived Talbot somewhat and he began to feel a little better and for a minute he stopped chasing the elusive memory of the voices he had heard while he lay sick and delirious in that shack. He turned to look at the Saville foreman. He supposed that aside from Jerome, Max was the closest thing he had to a friend.

'Thanks for pulling me out of there.'

Max turned to look at him briefly

and shook his head, laughing softly, because Talbot had already thanked him, several times.

'I don't remember much about it but thanks anyway. How did you find me?'

'You left a pretty good trail till the rain came. By then I'd an idea Gila had gone to the old Fletcher mine. I slipped past the lookout because of the storm, found a place to lie up for the day, watching the camp, and worked out that they had a prisoner in one of the buildings. I was just trying to figure out how to get you out of there when I had some help.'

'What do you mean?'

'A young girl, one of Francisco's girls I think, helped me, showed me a back way out of the camp.'

'The first time in my life I've been grateful to be ill,' Talbot said with a dry smile.

'How come?'

'Gila wanted me conscious. He wanted me to know what was going to happen to me. I was no use to him sick.' He tried to remember the girl but like so much of what had happened at the camp, she was just a blur.

'Well, I ain't gonna say I told you so.' Max hunched one shoulder and expertly turned the buggy into a handy space close to the railroad tracks. 'But I believe I did tell you to leave the lady where she was.'

But Talbot knew, as they began to walk up to the station platform, that Gila had only known of his involvement in the burial of his woman because somebody had told him. The thought surfaced gently, like a bubble in a beer glass, another little memory of the mining camp. Now all he had to do was remember why he had so urgently needed to be here.

The seven o'clock train was busy, the last westbound train out of Osborne until morning. A dozen or more waited on the platform to board and at least the same or more disembarked. In the confusion, a familiar stocky, bullet-necked figure stepped forward, thumbs in his belt, his hat tipped forward on his brow, scanning the incoming passengers without haste.

Max made a slight movement and Talbot rested a light hand on the foreman's arm. Murch was here to meet someone and he needed to know who.

The well-dressed, slightly portly man in his thirties who stepped forward, lowering his grip in order to shake Murch's hand, looked familiar but Talbot's sluggish brain could not connect the face with the memory. He had a little moustache that looked as if it had been drawn with a fine pencil and a pair of shrewd, deep-set brown eyes. Murch was explaining something and the other man nodded a touch impatiently, lifted his bag and indicated that they should leave the platform. Talbot turned to ask Max who he was and found that Doctor Jerome had joined them, his face angry and alarmed.

'What in the name of Christ are you

doing here?' he demanded furiously.

'I brung him,' Max explained, trying to deflect the doctor's anger away from the ashen-faced Talbot.

'Knowing how sick he is? In God's name why?'

'I'm all right, David. Don't blame Max. I just had to come to find out — ' He turned back to see where Murch and the other man had gone and instead saw another familiar face. One word dropped from his suddenly dry mouth.

'Irene.'

She could not have heard him above the noise of the departing train and yet at the exact moment he spoke her name she turned her head and their eyes met. He went to her, the thin queue of street-bound passengers obstructing him for an awkward moment before they met and embraced.

'Dearest, dearest,' she laughed and stroked her brother's dark hair and his pale cheek. He held her tightly for several minutes, eyes closed, inhaling the scent of her, a mixture of expensive French perfume and the more delicate rose face cream that she had always used.

Eventually he let her go and stepped back a little to let her say hello and exchange a warm greeting with Doctor Jerome, whom she had known all of her life. Then she turned back with glistening eyes to her brother.

She had noticed, even from a distance, the subtle change in him and close to now she saw that it was nearly all in the eyes. Physically he was much the same as she remembered, though not so well dressed of course, in faded blue work shirt and old pants and obviously not in very good health, but essentially the same man who had walked out of the house in a Union army uniform never to return. But there was a look in his eyes now, as if in some way he had been violated, his spirit grossly damaged and burnt out. It shocked her. She held on to his hand, unable to stop staring at him, realizing with another little jolt how like their father he had become.

'You've been ill,' she said. Her Boston accent thrilled him, her rich clothes and perfume intoxicated him with nostalgia for home.

'Just a little fever. I'm almost well again.'

'Is he all right, David?' she appealed to Jerome.

'He's been very sick and needs rest, lots of rest.'

'David says I might come and stay with him for a while. I'll take care of you. We can talk. I've such a lot to tell you.'

'You look wonderful.'

'Hardly dear, with four days soot on my face and my hair not combed since I don't know when.'

Soot or no she was a beautiful woman, as dark as her brother, with the same fine, graceful frame. Her 'uncombed' hair was dressed in a stylish chignon with a tiny, frivolous green and black velvet hat perched on one side of her head. She wore a dark green travelling dress and coat and had pearls at her ears and throat. She looked like a beautiful, exotic bird that had found its way from a foreign land.

'And this must be Max,' she said with a disarming smile at the Saville foreman, stepping up to him in a cloud of perfume. 'I'm Irene Talbot, Nathan's sister. I've heard so much about you.' She held out a hand and Max took it gingerly. She looked as if she were made of bone china.

'I never knew you had a sister, Nate,' Max complained, reluctantly releasing Irene's hand in its delicate kid glove.

'I have two sisters, Max.'

'Well if she's as beautiful as you — ' Max murmured. Irene laughed and diplomatically freed her hand, slipping an arm around her brother's waist.

'Nathan is the good-looking one of the family,' she insisted, but her eyes strayed to Doctor Jerome and Talbot was not too ill to notice.

'So this why you were here,' he said

to the doctor. 'Some surprise to spring on a sick man.'

'A nice surprise?' Irene asked, leaning against his arm. He looked down at her, scarcely able to believe that she was here.

'Yes,' he said softly, reaching down to kiss her cheek. 'The best tonic the doctor could have given me.'

23

Over supper in Doctor Jerome's parlour, the four of them sat around the table quietly talking, Irene asking questions and Nathan patiently answering. Few of his answers pleased her. When he told her about the menial work he had done when all their father's money lay waiting for him back East she was angry and hurt.

'Why didn't you come home?' she finally asked the question that had been on her lips all evening.

'Be sensible, Irene,' he said gently. 'Do you think Mother would have wanted me there?'

She looked down uncomfortably at the chicken on her plate and with a sigh put it away from her. She looked up and he was watching her closely.

'What is it?'

She pulled her chair closer to him

and put her hand on his shoulder.

'Oh my dear,' she murmured. 'Mother died in the spring. I didn't want the doctor to tell you till I could come myself.'

He leaned forward, his elbows on the table, his two hands clasped, pressed to his mouth. Irene stroked his back and looked helplessly at the doctor and an uncomfortable Max.

'She had a stroke,' Jerome explained. 'And before she could properly recover from it, she had another that killed her. That was one of the reasons I had those lawyers find you, Nate. I tried to tell you that first night in here, you remember, the night you got bur — ' A sharp kick under the table from Max stopped him from saying any more about what had been waiting for Talbot in the livery barn that night and with a rueful cough, Jerome fell silent.

Nathan tried to find some soft, kind memory of his mother with which to bury her but could not. She had always been cool and distant and unmotherly to him, had never held or kissed him or shown him by a single word or look that she cared for him. His stock of memories of his mother was bankrupt.

After Cherry Bridge he had written to her to tell her what had happened. Her reply had hurt but not surprised him. She simply told him that he had damaged his family's good name for ever, that she never wanted to see him again, and that if he returned to Boston, his sister's lives would be ruined. Clearly, Irene didn't know that her mother had written such a letter and he had no mind to tell her. Yet now, perversely, he felt a painful ache that he would never see her again, never hear her flat-voweled, no-nonsense voice, never feel irritated by her ambition and interference in his life.

'You didn't have to travel all this way to tell me, sweetheart.'

'I know, but there's something else. Dolly was engaged to be married when Mother died and now they've decided to go ahead with their plans.'

'Dolly engaged?' Talbot shook his head, remembering a girl who changed her mind about her beaux by the hour.

'To Jack Lawson. Do you remember him?'

He nodded uncertainly, recalling a gaunt, serious young man with a prominent Adam's apple, the very last person he would have expected his flighty young sister to choose.

'She wants you there, to give her away. And, of course, Mother left a good deal of property and so on to you, dear, and we need you to come home and sort everything out. Uncle Matthew has been looking after things but — '

'No,' he said curtly and he reached for the decanter to pour himself a drink, ignoring Doctor Jerome's strictures about liquor until he was completely well. 'I don't belong there anymore.'

'Well, you don't belong here either,' Irene said with an apologetic glance at the other two men in the room. 'From what David has told me you can't even go back to that ranch. Those men tried to kill you. You have nothing here.'

Max and Jerome sat on the sidelines, engrossed, silent, not taking sides. Max could have told the beautiful young lady that her brother had one very important thing to stay for but Nathan would not have appreciated it. And Doctor Jerome quietly watched the unmistakable signs of returning fever and approaching collapse in his young friend.

'The war is over. People have forgotten,' Irene tried to assure him.

'I haven't.'

'Well, I know that, darling. I know you can't forget all those men on that bridge and all but, if you can't forget then it shouldn't matter where you live.'

She was willing to badger and hurt him if it made him see sense. She wanted him home, all the family did.

'Why did you have to bring her here?' Talbot asked Jerome and the doctor raised his eyebrows and moved the whiskey decanter out of his reach.

'Because you had no right to declare yourself dead,' Jerome responded almost angrily. 'There were people back in Boston who cared for you, wanted you home, and I thought your sister might be able to persuade you of that fact.'

'Come home, Nathan,' she coaxed him, 'even if it's just long enough to give Dolly away and sort out Mother's affairs.'

He turned to look at his young sister and he remembered how shy and timid she used to be. On those few occasions when his mother had insisted that he take her with him on some outing, she had clung to him, afraid of the horses and the rough sailors on their father's ships, shy of his friends. He always scorned her fears and laughed at her shyness, but he never let go of her hand, or let anything or anyone hurt her. He had bloodied the nose of one of his friends when he had rudely called her a simpleton. Now she had travelled across half a continent to find him, alone, unchaperoned, in order to reclaim her prodigal brother. For a girl raised in polite Boston society, sheltered from all that was cruel and unpleasant in the world, that was quite something. And at that moment Irene saw his resistance collapse.

'I always thought not going home was the best for everyone concerned,' he said to her and she quietly sighed and shook her head.

'No, dearest. You were wrong for once.'

'All right then,' he agreed.

'When he's well enough to travel,' Jerome cautioned and Irene laughed.

'I've waited all these years. I can be patient a little longer.' She started to rise from her chair and all three men rose with her. 'I think I'd like to go to bed now. It's been quite a day. It was lovely to meet you, Max,' she smiled at the foreman and then turned to Doctor Jerome, giving him her hand and looking at him with a little of her former shyness. 'Goodnight, David.

Thank you for letting me stay.'

Jerome bowed formally over her hand and then smiled at her. For a moment the two of them were unaware of anyone else in the room before she lowered her eyes and turned to say goodnight to her brother, squeezing him tightly around the middle and kissing him.

'Are you glad I came?' she asked and he nodded and tucked a stray curl of dark hair behind her ear.

'I am. Get some rest. We'll talk some more in the morning.'

When she was out of the room all three sat down again.

'You are full of surprises, David,' Talbot said, giving his friend a meaningful look which Jerome chose to ignore. He got up again and went into his medical bag. He mixed a little white powder in a wine glass of water and placed it on the table before him. Talbot drank the familiar bitter mixture without protest.

'If I'd known you were going to come

down with a bout I wouldn't have let her come. And I don't want her presence to interfere with your getting well. That little stunt tonight for example.' And he looked meaningfully at Max. Max put on an air of injured innocence.

'He was dead set on it, Doc. Seemed to me the best thing to do was to humour him, take him in the buggy and see he was OK.'

'What I want to know is what was so all-fired important that you had to leave a sick bed to take care of it?' Jerome directed his question at Talbot. 'Why tonight? Why that train in particular?'

Talbot sat still and silent so long, staring at the wine glass he still held, that the doctor and Max exchanged worried looks. Then he pulled a big breath down into his chest and looked up at his two friends, a rueful smile on his tired face.

'I don't know, David. Something I heard . . . a snatch of conversation at the mining camp. All I could remember was the train time and the day. But there was nothing out of the way at the station, was there, Max?'

'We saw Ray Murch,' Max reminded him, his tone implying that Murch should have been dealt with a long time since, but Talbot just stared at Max, with that unblinking gaze that was so disconcerting.

'Who was that man he met off the train?' he asked.

'His name is Mason. He arrived about a year ago, bought over a few concerns, the hotel, the saloon on Gold Street,' Doctor Jerome answered. He had seen the two men at the station just before he saw Max and Talbot.

'Rumour has it he put up the money for the fancy house at the back of the railroad tracks,' Max chipped in and the doctor gave Max a long hard look. He sincerely hoped that the foreman was not frequenting Mason's brothel. He spent a lot of time telling patients to drop their pants so that he could inspect the consequences.

Talbot's eyelids drooped as the

medicine began to take effect. He wished that he could remember. His brain felt as if it had been pan-broiled.

'Time for bed,' Jerome ordered gently and, with a nod, Talbot pushed himself to his feet. He got into bed with a hand from Jerome, barely able to keep his eyes open, even when the doctor took his pulse.

'I don't want any more nonsense from you, Nathan. You don't rise from this bed till I say different. You hear me?'

Talbot gave a tiny nod, closed his eyes and let himself drift. At Cherry Bridge Corporal Roberts offered him a boost, helping him into the saddle.

'He's had a big day,' Max observed from the foot of the bed.

'Irene was a shock to him.'

'She was a shock to all of us,' Max laughed softly and the doctor smiled too, but in a different way from Max.

'He's got to rest now. I'm counting on Irene to make him stay put for a day or two.'

'I wonder what it was he overheard at

the mining camp,' Max said almost to himself as they returned to the parlour.

'You want to bed down here for the night, Max? I can let you have the couch. It's late to be riding back.'

'Nah, Louise'll only worry. And the brat would probably come looking for me,' he grinned, knowing that Trisa was capable of doing just that. 'Night, Doc. I'll look in day after tomorrow, see how Nathan is doing.'

When he was gone, the front door locked, lights dimmed, the house quiet but for the measured workings of the old half-case clock on the wall, Doctor Jerome sat down at the table and poured himself a nightcap, his thoughts turning to the woman sleeping in the guest room, the woman he had loved since she was about twelve years old. The secret thrill he felt knowing she was here, under his roof, was almost painful in its intensity.

They had been writing to one another for years now, since before the war. Her letters were sweet, funny, insightful and with the passage of time, increasingly intimate. Now she was sleeping in his mother's bed, which he had shipped out from home, curled up under his finest Irish linen sheets, covered by his grandmother's prized patchwork comforter. His mind wandered down that unproductive alley of sheets and nightgowns and soft mattresses until he pulled himself back to reality and swallowed his whiskey. Yes, it was wonderful to see her, to hear her, to be close enough to touch her. But what would he do when she went home?

He heard a sound and turned his head, thinking it was Nathan, awake and needing him, and saw Irene, standing in the doorway. She wore a thin silk robe over her nightdress, her dark hair falling in soft curls over her shoulders. He stared at her for a minute or more, then put his glass down and opened his arms. Without hesitation she went to him, letting him fold her into his embrace as if it was the most natural place in the world for her to be.

24

Two days later Talbot felt strong enough to walk down the main street with Irene on his arm, to show her the few shops and carry her parcels of ribbon and calico. The general store held her captive for an hour and then they walked back, as she sensed that her brother was flagging. As they came through the door to the doctor's front parlour, they saw that Jerome had a visitor. Talbot had forgotten what a jolt the sight of her could give him.

Trisa, balancing on the arm of one of the doctor's chairs, turned and saw them come in, the beautiful and beautifully dressed young woman with her arm around Nathan, leaning on him, laughing up into his face. Her first sight of him since that never-to-be-forgotten night when he brought her world down like a house of cards and he had another woman with him, holding on to him as if she owned him. She knew she was just his sister but nevertheless Trisa felt an acute spasm of jealousy, especially since she knew she looked a fright in jeans and work shirt, her hair poked up under her hat to keep out the grain dust, for she had been helping Max and two of the hands load feed into a wagon. Compared to the woman in the fashionable blue dress she knew she looked like an old squaw.

'Are you looking for Doctor Jerome?' Irene asked pleasantly. 'He had to go out on a call.'

'I came to see Nathan,' Trisa said and Irene gave her brother a surprised smile.

'Irene, this is Mr Saville's daughter, Trisa. Trisa, this is my sister, Irene.'

'How do you do?' Irene continued in the same pleasant tone, while her brother and the young girl stood looking at one another in silence. Trisa was shocked to see how pale and ill Talbot looked, great dark patches of exhaustion under his eyes, as if he hadn't slept in a month. She swallowed her pity. She swallowed it and saved it for her dead brother.

'We can talk in here,' Talbot said, indicating the bedroom he had been using. He did not look at his sister. He knew she would be shocked to her hair roots to see him take a young lady into a bedroom. The blind was still half-drawn in here and there were warm shadows and odd patterns of light and shade in what had been Talbot's sick room.

'Why did you have to come here?' Trisa opened up, her voice much angrier, much more hostile than before. Talbot didn't answer at first, but just allowed himself a long look at her.

'Your family seemed to be in such trouble. I just wanted to help, to try to make amends.'

'What could you possibly do to make amends for killing my brother?' she demanded. With this Talbot fell silent. He would not argue with her or plead his cause. He waited to hear her condemnation, her justified condemnation with a tense, tired face and folded arms.

'I could kill you,' she said fiercely. 'I hate you enough to kill you. I wish I'd let Jack Spinner alone that night.' Her voice was almost breaking as she hurled her abuse at him, the words she'd rehearsed in her head a hundred times pitched at him through clenched teeth and rigid jaw. But all the time she was thinking, why didn't he look like a villain, like the monster her brother's killer had to be?

'But you saved my life and you saved the ranch and my dad and — ' Her lips began to tremble. She put her hand to her mouth and her eyes filled with hot tears. She began to weep uncontrollably, her tears turning to sobs that shook her bodily. Distressed now, Talbot lightly gripped her shoulder.

'Trisa, sweetheart, please don't — '

She pulled free of his touch, ashamed of his seeing her tears.

'I'm all right,' she said hoarsely, giving him an unforgiving, wet-lashed look and using her sleeve to scrub her face clean.

She reached into her pocket and took out the locket he had given her and, not even wanting to touch his hand, put it down on the dresser. But she couldn't bear to part from him like this, no matter what he'd done, couldn't bear to part from him at all. She had been telling Nathan Talbot for months that she was not a child, that she was as mature as a woman can be, old enough for him. But just now she felt about twelve years old. Her initial anger had evaporated, leaving her unbearably sad.

Without another word she went to him and put her arms around his waist, rested her head for a minute on his shoulder, then reached up and kissed his mouth. Before Talbot could respond, hold her, say anything, she had slipped away and was gone from the room. When he looked up his sister was standing in the doorway, watching him anxiously.

She came into the room and her eye was caught by the locket on the dresser. She lifted it and looked at Talbot's white, unhappy face.

'You gave her grandmother's locket?'

'Yes. It was my birthday gift to her some weeks ago.'

'My dear, I think you and I ought to talk.'

'By all means,' Talbot said, taking her by the arm and guiding her gently to the door. 'And perhaps you can explain to me what you and David Jerome were doing in the parlour the other night after I went to bed.'

Irene gave a gasp of shock and stopped, turning to stare at Nathan, but a reply of any kind escaped her.

'Idiot,' he smiled at her. 'David Jerome's been in love with you since you were twelve years old. I just wondered how long it would take you to realize you felt the same. I hope he's going to make an honest woman of you.'

'Yes,' she said with a shaky laugh. 'He

. . . he has asked me to marry him. David wanted to wait until you were well again before speaking to you.'

'I'm well enough for good news. He won't go back to Boston you know, Irene,' he told her quietly.

'I know. We've talked about it. I've told him I want to be where he is. And I rather like Caldwell. I think it's growing into a decent little town.' She smiled at her brother, vastly relieved that it was not a secret any more and that Nathan approved, was glad for her.

'You know, I was a little worried about seeing David again after all these years. I thought he might have acquired several chins or a little pot belly, or be wearing gold-rimmed eye-glasses. Silly of me, because the minute I saw him I knew it wouldn't have made a bit of difference how he looked.'

Talbot stared at her, arrested by what she had said, trying to connect her words with a recent event.

'Well, that's love for you,' he smiled at her.

'You look tired out, dear. Why don't you have a rest till suppertime? I'll call you.'

As she closed the door, Talbot turned for the bed, sinking back on to it, pleased with himself for having deflected Irene from any discussion about Trisa. He wished she had kept the locket though. He slept till late in the afternoon, and when he woke, his mind was quite clear at last. He had made the connection.

Jerome was still out on his rounds when he let himself into his office. The doctor's files, kept behind a glass fronted book case, were like the man himself, neat and orderly, each file clearly marked and dated. The one he wanted came readily enough to his hand, labelled 'Correspondence regarding Cherry Bridge'.

Talbot sat down behind the doctor's desk, opened the file and immediately found what he was looking for, a single sheet of paper with the list of names of the men who had died on the bridge, name and rank, the list David Jerome had used when he wrote to the men's families. Talbot ran his index finger down the neat column of names till he found the one he wanted.

He stared at it and felt a thrill of recognition, his finger pressing down so hard on the ink that it smudged. For some minutes, he sat perfectly still, letting the significance of his find sink in and then he closed the file and put it back where he had found it. Making his way back upstairs in search of his promised supper he realized that for the first time in an age he had an appetite.

25

Murch was late. The man who had hired him and Francisco and the others, consulted his expensive gold watch for the twentieth time and impatiently got up to look out of the window of the parlour of his opulent Osborne home. Murch was over an hour late, and if he didn't come for the gold, then Francisco would take his little travelling circus and go. He had come too far, invested too much for that.

He turned and walked out of the parlour, crossed the hallway and opened the door to his private study. It was not too late to take the gold himself. He lit the lamp on the desk and unlocked the bottom drawer, withdrawing the dozen or so small leather bags, filled with Francisco's final payment. Then he paused. Something wasn't right. He opened the drawer again and looked for the object that was always kept there and at the same moment, heard the creak of leather and looked up into the muzzle of his own gun.

'Looking for this?' Talbot asked, leaning forward slightly into the light. He edged a hip on to the desk and rested the gun on his forearm. 'Corporal Roberts, isn't it?' he asked quietly. 'Corporal Mason Roberts?'

Roberts nodded, badly shaken by this turn of events. His heart was pumping so hard he felt Talbot must be able to hear it.

'I saw you at the railroad station, but I didn't recognize you at first. Then someone made a remark about how people can change over the years and I remembered you. You've let yourself go, Corporal.'

Talbot noted the expensive tailored coat and embroidered waistcoat, the soft linen and the gold rings on Roberts's hand. Roberts looked what he was, a rich, respectable businessman, gone a little soft with easy living. 'Don't misunderstand my next question, Roberts, but, why aren't you dead?'

'Believe me, Captain, I didn't want to involve you in any of this.'

'I don't hold the rank of captain any longer,' Talbot reminded him. Roberts simply stared at him, as if he, Talbot, were the ghost at the proceedings. 'Is that gold meant for Francisco, to finish off the Saville ranch?' he asked and Roberts nodded slowly.

'I made a mistake, didn't I, letting you live? I should have let Castle kill you, like he wanted to.'

'Yes, you made a bad mistake and I wouldn't bother looking for Murch to come,' Talbot said, seeing Roberts's eyes dart towards the little clock on the desk for the third time.

'Where is he?' Roberts asked and was annoyed that his voice sounded slightly breathless.

'He's been taken care of,' Talbot said, recalling with satisfaction how he and Max Ryan had ambushed Murch in

Roberts's stables. Max had nearly killed him before Talbot restrained him. Now he was trussed and gagged and waiting his fate. Talbot leaned forward slightly and Roberts could see the effects of his recent illness, his pallor and the bruised skin under his eyes.

'Now perhaps you'd like to tell me what really happened at Cherry Bridge?'

Roberts leaned back slightly, hands on the desk top, wondering what Talbot would make of what he had to say.

'What really happened was that Howard cut the fuse short on you. You didn't kill anybody, Captain. It was all planned.' Roberts looked at Talbot for a reaction to being told he hadn't caused those men's deaths, expecting shock, anger maybe, but Talbot's face was completely expressionless. And yet Roberts had never felt such a sense of menace emanating from another human being.

'What really happened was that Howard saw the dispatch before you did, the dispatch that told him that there was a haul of rebel gold coming back with one of those scouting parties. Howard decided it was time to cut short his army career and he asked me to go along with him.'

'So when you found the scouting party with the gold, you relieved them of it and sent them back over the bridge,' Talbot finished for him.

'We told them how to signal you, said it was just to let you know they were coming. But it was your signal to blow the bridge.'

'With them on it.'

'With them on it,' Roberts admitted candidly, no remorse, no shame. 'Howard and me took the money and headed south-west.'

'I take it Howard betrayed you, took the gold for himself?' Talbot guessed and Roberts laughed.

'I should have known better than to trust him. He knocked me out cold two days later. But he wasn't content just to leave me and take the gold. He dressed himself in a Confederate uniform and

273

handed me over to a Southern unit, told them I was a spy. He watched them stand me up against a barn and shoot me. Two bullets in the leg, one in my chest. The rest missed me. When I woke up I was in Andersonville. Another company had found me, patched me up.'

Talbot felt no sympathy. Roberts had allowed those men to ride on to Cherry Bridge knowing they would die, and he had given the word for the murders and attempted murders at the Saville place.

'You seem to have done all right for yourself,' he said.

'I won a hotel in a card game. There was plenty of money to be made in the south at the end of hostilities. I spent two years making good, buying other hotels, a freight line, a saloon here and there. I found I had a head for business.'

'But you wanted to get even with Howard.'

'You have a gift for understatement, Captain. Yes, I wanted to get even and more. I finally found him in Mexico. I didn't kill him though. Francisco caught him dealing from the bottom of the deck and put a bullet through his brain. He had spent the gold, every last ounce of it. You were always right about him, Captain. He never did amount to anything.'

'But you still wanted revenge. You wanted his father's ranch.'

'Howard always said one day he'd come back here, turn up like the prodigal son, saying he'd been wounded or some such and claim his birthright. So that was all I had left. To take away what Howard should have had. Then you turned up. I told them all you weren't to be harmed. I did that at least for you,' he insisted.

'Thanks,' Talbot broached a dry smile.

'You know if Howard had just held on, waited for the outcome at Cherry Bridge, he would have got his promotion on your coat-tails. You were just an ordinary captain but you'd been noticed.

You would have been breveted major at least, maybe colonel. Just being mentioned in the same breath as you would have helped his career, but he couldn't see it. You were just somebody always holding him back, holding him down.'

Talbot turned his body slightly, though his eyes and the gun never moved from Roberts's face.

'Did you catch any of that, sir?' he asked the darkness. Roberts leaned forward slightly, mystified. Walking slowly but without the cane he had been using recently, Greg Saville moved out of the shadows at the back of the room. He had listened to Roberts's story and now his was the face of a man who had had the worst news possible, the devastating news that his son was a thief, a liar and a murderer.

He had come here tonight in response to a note from Talbot asking him if he wanted to hear some news of his son. And now he had heard it and he almost wished he hadn't. He rested his hand on Talbot's shoulder.

'It was hard to hear it, but I'm glad I came.' Saville looked at Roberts, the muscles of his face still stiff with anger. 'I'm sorry my son did what he did to you, but the men who died on my ranch because of your vendetta had no part in that, nor did my daughter, an innocent child, nearly raped and murdered on your order. How can you possibly justify that?'

Roberts retreated into stubborn silence. His skin had taken on a greasy hue and was slick with perspiration and his heart was tripping unevenly. He had not felt himself to be in this much danger since the night in Andersonville when he had gotten into a knife fight with a half-starved soldier called Mullins.

'What are we going to do with him?' Saville asked and suddenly Roberts acted.

He stood up, lifting the desk with him, shoving it forward. The edge of it kicked the pistol out of Talbot's hand and he twisted, accidentally knocking Saville to the floor. Roberts flung open the study door and was half way across the hallway when Talbot caught up with him, yanking him back into a hard punch to the body. Roberts struck back, his fist hitting Talbot on the side of the head and shoulder, but nothing that counted. Talbot stamped hard on the inside of Roberts's instep and then jabbed an elbow into the other man's throat. He fell, taking Talbot with him and they rolled towards the stairs that led to the upstairs rooms. Roberts, on his back, had got his hands around Talbot's throat and was squeezing hard, thumbs digging into his windpipe. Talbot retaliated, a fist under Roberts's jaw, forcing the other man's head back at an impossible angle. Then unexpectedly, Roberts started to gasp and gulp for air, his eyes round with fright and his two fists slackening and falling away from Talbot's neck.

Talbot, straddling the other man, rolled to one side, understanding at once what was happening. He tugged

Roberts's necktie loose and opened the collar of his shirt, reached down lower and loosened his belt and the waist of his pants, while Roberts's eyes pleaded for help and his face began to mottle and then turn alarmingly grey.

'I . . . tried to save you. Howard betrayed us both. I just wanted — '

A moment later he was dead. Talbot saw the life in his eyes fade and heard the last breath gurgle from his throat. His head rolled to one side, his eyes staring towards the door he had been trying to reach.

Talbot looked up and Saville was there, surprised to see Roberts obviously dead after what had in actual fact been only a matter of one or two minutes. He sank down on to the lowest tread of the stairs and Talbot sat down beside him. Saville looked with some concern at his young partner, for Talbot's colour was no better than Roberts's.

'Heart attack, I think,' Talbot explained nodding to the dead man. 'I saw the same thing happen once before.'

'You knew he was going to say some of that, didn't you?' Saville said quietly. 'That's why you sent for me tonight.'

'Well, Roberts had somehow survived Cherry Bridge and now he was here, causing all your problems. Why? He was clearly bent on revenge. Why against you? He didn't know you. So I guessed it must be something to do with Howard. Why would he want revenge on Howard if he died on Cherry Bridge? Again I was just guessing, but I figured if Roberts was alive then probably Howard was too. I'm sorry I was wrong about that.'

'Killed in a dirty poker game,' Saville ground out, shaking his head. 'When he was ten years old his mother predicted something like that would happen to him. I denied it to myself for twenty odd years but I kept hoping I might be wrong. But he was bad through and through, born that way. Only Trisa ever saw any good in him.'

'It's all in the past now. Nobody ever

needs to know about any of this but you and me.' Talbot said meaningfully.

'But everybody is going to know, son. I'll make sure of that. You think I care about my son's reputation after what I heard tonight in this room?'

'What about Trisa?' he asked quietly. 'What happens when she finds out the truth about her brother?'

'She's a big girl now, Nathan, at least that's what she keeps telling everybody,' Saville said with a rueful smile.

'I can't let you do that to her, sir.'

'You love her that much?' Saville asked and unexpectedly Talbot flushed. He had spent so much time keeping his feelings to himself that Saville's words took him aback.

'I'm going back to Boston and she can get on with her life here. She won't know about Howard and . . . she'll forget me. Somebody else will come along.'

Saville smiled his first genuine smile in months. His world, if not exactly righted, was at least starting to tilt that way. And if he were honest, he couldn't think of anyone he would rather trust his daughter to. He didn't think Trisa would give Talbot up that easily, but he was willing to concede the argument for now.

'What are we going to do about him?' he asked nodding towards Roberts.

'We have to try to make it look natural. If the sheriff suspects we were here he'll make trouble.'

They posed Roberts in his chair behind the desk, with a pen and some papers under his hand and rearranged the disordered room. They were about to leave when Talbot lifted the bags of gold and handed them to Saville. He saw that Saville was about to protest but fiercely stopped him.

'This gold was to be paid tonight to a man who intended to destroy you. We're not leaving it here for Roberts's crooked sheriff to find or his crooked lawyer or bank manager or anybody else he had in his pocket. This is going in your safe, to help pay for the bunkhouse and the broken fencing and everything else, all right?'

Saville hadn't the energy to argue with him. He nodded tiredly.

'We have to move Murch,' Talbot said. 'We'll take him to Caldwell. I just have one question to ask him, one more thing I need to know.'

'What's that?'

'I want to know the name of Gila's woman, the girl who died?'

'I know that,' Saville said. 'It was Mary.' He started to turn towards the door, then stopped and turned back to look at Talbot. 'But her family always called her Lark.'

The very last piece of the puzzle fell into place, the last fragment of memory of the dying girl and of the mining camp. Talbot remembered now how Murch had boasted of killing both the girl and Jud Willis. He reached into his pocket for his bill-fold and removed the object that Trisa had given him the day Jud died, the broken chain with the little bird. As he held it up to the light, the talisman spun and twisted just as if it wanted to fly.

The sky was just beginning to lighten when Gila returned to the cabin he had shared with his wife since they came here. It was less than a mile from Osborne, at the end of a disused track, with a good fresh water supply and a little wooded area at the back where there was always plenty of fresh game. His wife had been half white and she liked to be near the town. He would have cut down the moon for her if she wanted.

Bitterness and impotent rage churned inside him. Today. He would settle with Talbot today, before they pulled stakes and went south again. Murch hadn't come with the money. Francisco was already gone.

He circled the cabin to the corral to see to his horse and as he turned the corner he came to a dead stop. A man was tied to the corral poles, his arms bent over the top spar and lashed, his legs tied to the lower rails. He was gagged, none too gently and his upper body and feet were bare.

It was Ray Murch tied to his corral rail and his eyes were bulging with terror. It took Gila another minute to work out why. Tied around Murch's neck was a broken chain that had been crudely knotted to repair the break, and on the chain, the talisman that he had given to his wife on their joining day, a small silver bird in flight, meant to represent her name: Lark. Behind the gag, Murch whimpered.

26

They all came to see them off on their journey back to Boston, Max, Louise, Dr Jerome, Greg Saville. And Trisa.

She had gone back to looking like the girl he had first seen in Casey's livery barn, a shotgun in her arms. Her short hair clung in damp tendrils to her temples and her grey, grown-up eyes were slitted against a hot, dry wind coming in up the rail track. She wore a plaid shirt, the sleeves rolled up past her elbows. It was a red shirt, Talbot deliberately noted and her jeans were an old black pair that had faded to grey. According to Saville, she had taken the news about her brother a lot more calmly than anyone expected. But still, Talbot knew it must have been hard on her.

She watched with hostility and pretended indifference as he kissed

Louise and hugged Max and the doctor and shook Saville's hand. Her father gripped him by the shoulder, acknowledging the debt he owed him. She folded her arms and watched his astonishingly beautiful and sophisticated sister take her farewells, exchanging a teasing word with Max, kissing Louise, smiling warmly at Greg Saville and wishing him a speedy and full recovery. She had said her private goodbyes to David the night before, now she kissed him and whispered something to which David Jerome softly laughed, the love and affection they felt for one another plain and for Trisa, painful to see. Suddenly she turned and was gone before either one could say anything kind or patronizing to her, before she had to endure his final Judas kiss on the cheek.

Talbot, seeing that she was gone, looked stricken for a moment. Irene touched his hand, though privately she understood why Trisa had left. Max shook his head and said she was just a wild kid at times and Saville promised she wouldn't sit down for a week, whether she was twenty or not. Louise said nothing, smiled to herself and said she thought it was time they got on the train.

Irene was seated and the baggage stored in a few minutes and then Talbot came to stand on the observation platform to wave sadly to some people who had become family to him. He found he could scarcely endure leaving them.

'Come back and see us, Nathan,' Louise called out to him.

'Boston's too damp for your health,' Jerome reminded him.

'I never did tell you what happened to that milk cow,' Max shouted as the train picked up speed and his last glimpse was of them laughing which was better than seeing them look as sad as he felt. If only Trisa had not bolted. And yet he was glad. What on earth could he have said to her with everyone there? He stood for a while watching the town and then the prairie, the grass dry and yellow, bending to the hot, dusty wind.

'Nathan?' He whirled around to find Trisa standing on a corner of the observation platform.

'What in the world are you doing here?'

'It's OK; there's a water stop about four miles up the line. Max is gonna wait for me.'

He stared at her in exasperation, and then leaned back against the railing, just looking as the breeze stirred her hair.

'I don't want you to go,' she said bluntly.

'I have to go Trisa. My sister is being married.'

'We need you more than she does.'

'I have to take care of my father's business. I should have gone home a long time ago.'

'This is your home now,' she argued. She came to stand beside him, to harangue him at close quarters. 'This is where you belong.'

He continued to gaze at her with a look of tender longing, but shook his head. He still believed that she was a child, that she would change her mind a dozen times before settling down with some lanky cowboy. Much as he wanted her, much as he needed her, he had to make one more sacrifice.

'I belong in Boston,' he said, trying to harden his tone. 'And that's where I'm going.' He turned away from the intense pain in her eyes, saying hoarsely, 'You'll soon forget all about me. You'll meet someone else.'

'No,' she said furiously. 'I won't. I'll never love anyone else but you. I'm not a kid any more.'

'Trisa, I'm going home to see my sister married, to give her away. Do you want to know how many times she was in love at your age?'

'But I'm not her. I'm me. I'm not like that.'

He knew that was true. In some things, a lot of things, she was vastly more mature than most young women of his acquaintance.

'All right, Trisa. If you still feel the same way in a year's time, you come to Boston and find me, bring me back.'

That silenced her. The sudden breach in the stone wall of his resistance took her by surprise. She moistened her lips and thought about it, a year without him. But if that was what it took.

'Do you mean it?' she asked. He looked pale at having so impulsively committed himself but nodded.

'When you're twenty-one, old enough to know what you want.'

'I come to Boston.' The idea appalled her.

'Doctor Jerome knows where I live. He's going to try to find someone to take over his practice for a few months so that he can come and marry Irene in Boston. Come with him. Bring Louise, bring Max and your dad too if you want.'

'And then bring you back.'

'Yes. If that's what you still want.'

'What . . . what if it's not what you

want?' she said hesitantly.

'I'm not going to change my mind about you, Trisa,' he said softly and he took her into his arms, settled one hand low on her back and brought the other up to gently cup her breast and then kissed her the way he had always wanted to kiss her, a slow, lingering, intense, intimate exploration that left Trisa breathless, her legs trembling.

The train had begun to slow. Reluctantly he let her slip from his arms, drew one last breath of her skin and hair, took one last look into her eyes, wide with surprise at the evidence of Talbot's desire and then watched her climb over the observation rail, dropping easily down on to the ground as the train came to a brief halt. She stood looking up at him, intently studying his face.

'You better not forget,' she warned him. He just nodded. Then he reached up around his neck, removed his grandmother's locket, and threw it down to her.

'I won't,' he said as the train jerked forward, moving slowly at first. 'Goodbye, Trisa.'

Talbot lifted his head to scan the horizon, watching for Max. When he saw the Saville foreman in the distance, leading Trisa's horse, he looked down at her again and raised one hand in farewell.

She walked along after the train for a while, watching him fiercely, trying to remember every detail of him. His clothes were the ones he'd worn to her birthday party, clean white shirt, black high button vest and pants, black neck tie. He was still pale from his fever and the breeze gently ruffled the dark strands of his hair as he looked back at her, hands resting on the guard rail.

'You better not forget,' she said again and she stopped, reaching up with two hands to fasten his locket. 'Because I'll be on your doorstep in a year's time, Nathan Talbot.'

COMANCHERO TRAIL

Jack Dakota

For the new hired gun at the Rafter W, the owner's wilful granddaughter, Miss Trashy, is the first of his troubles. Dean Kittredge must then face El Serpiente and his gang of Comanchero outlaws, backed by Jensen Crudace, the land and cattle agent who plans to control the territory. Kittredge and ranch foreman Tad Sherman track down El Serpiente to his hidden base in the heart of a distant mesa. Will they succeed in stopping the ruthless gunmen?

SOFT SOAP FOR A HARD CASE

Billy Hall

Sam Heller had been hit — hampered in his speed of drawing and holding a gun. He and a homesteader faced Lance Russell and his trusty sidekick when they stepped out from behind a shed. Two against two, yet Sam didn't have a chance: he would always struggle to out-draw them. Meanwhile, Kate Bond waited, hoping for his return, whilst her beloved Sam was determined to go down fighting. Then Russell and his hired gunmen went for their guns . . .